# Cinema

# CINEMA

SAMUEL KAYE

Whisk(e)y Tit
VT & NYC

Published in the United States by Whisk(e)y Tit www.whiskeytit.com. If you wish to use or reproduce all or part of this book for any means, please let the author and publisher know. You're pretty much required to, legally.

ISBN 978-1-952600-02-9

Library of Congress Control Number: 9781952600029



Cover design by Julia Suter.

First Whisk(e)y Tit paperback edition.

# ADVANCE PRAISE

Samuel Kaye is a Kafka for these neoliberal, fame-obsessed times. But he is a better writer than the Bohemian. His crisp, taut prose and flat characters create a world where there is no authentic self, but merely layers of performance. So much so, that it is not stretching it to say that performance is the main character and method of this novel. The book itself is performative. It performs what it is about in its structure and unfolding. It does what it says. Kaye enacts the arguments he describes. He mounts classic debates in performance studies around how an actor should act, specifically mentioning Diderot, Stanislavski, and Strasberg, and brings down a conclusion something like Mamet, where the actor serves the writing, allowing it to bring itself to life through its takeover of the actor's body. Kaye also stretches this to build a world where the various meanings of performance, from the aesthetic performance of the actors, the neoliberal jargon of corporate performance, and the everyday performance of self blend into each other. He shows how these various modes of performance manifest as languages. In this, he reveals the nuanced complexity of self which has historically been variously misinterpreted as soul, psyche, and subject, to be performance. The media-constructed real-world actors he writes about, his interpretation of them as characters in the novel, the real world and fictional characters they play in the film in the novel, and the imaginary characters the writer-director constructs on them in their imaginations, blend effortlessly into each other in a play of revealing and obscuring, appearing and disappearing. This is further complexified by the multi-faceted dimensions of the characters portrayed in the novel playing characters in the film bleeding into the characters in the novel being written in the film being made in the novel. Through this layering, Kaye circumscribes the limit where self and performance become each other. This is important work. Fucken capital L literature. But this is not just a novel. It is philosophy in a way to which so many novels pretend but fail. Enjoyable though it is, this book should not be merely enjoyed, but studied as the performance of philosophy of performance which it is.

Dr. Stuart Grant, Senior Lecturer, Centre for Theatre and Performance, Monash University

# CINEMA

---

It had been a long month of report writing, business planning, and client engagement. There were always peaks and troughs, with the downturns accompanied by messages from the executive about changing the way we were working, increasing productivity, and being more consultative. We were now in the middle of a lull, hopefully before things picked up again. Times of slower than usual business activity lowered team morale. There wasn't much to do and it gave rise to a lack of enthusiasm for work, work friendships, and the future. It also gave staff, I think, an opportunity to consider their long-term futures and position themselves to be kept on no matter what happened.

I suppose that's what office work is all about—Machiavellian manoeuvres to ensure your survival. I didn't put enough thought or planning into my career as I should have. Someone once said to me, *you really need to think about your performance and how you come across.*

I was considering these things standing at the printer waiting for some reports, when one of the directors introduced me to a new employee. She couldn't have been more than twenty-five. She was starting in the contracts team. I didn't know we were taking on new people. The message from above had always been *things were pretty tight* so I thought it more likely some of us would be let go. Just as we were about to start a conversation, the printer jammed and the red lights came on.

I thought it was going to be awkward but the situation turned out to be an ice-breaker. The new girl laughed—*well doesn't that always happen?*

The director was in a hurry to get to a meeting that had already started, no doubt nervous he may miss something important. He was carrying a giant takeaway coffee. The director asked whether I could introduce the new girl, Claire, to the rest of the floor. After he'd hurried off, she leant over the machine and read out the model name and number—*Ricoh RMFD780*. Claire knew the model and asked if I'd mind if she had a look. I told her to be my guest because I was hopeless with them. I lightheartedly remarked how they only seem to break down when I'm near them.

Claire knelt down and opened a panel. She pulled a lever, looked inside, and told me the machine was the first of *Ricoh's* new generation of multi-function devices—they'd done a complete redesign. She reached in and pulled out the paper that had caused the blockage. The warning lights went off and she shut the doors. The machine shook. The display told us it was cleaning itself and we should wait.

Unfortunately, as soon as the self-cleaning operation had finished, the warning lights came on again. I suggested the paper jam, although cleared, had perhaps caused a more serious problem. Claire asked what brand of paper the company used. I said I'd never noticed. I walked to the compactus where the paper was stored and showed her a new ream. She shook her head and frowned.

"You should never use generic-brand paper on complicated, multi-function devices," she said. "Even if you fan out the sheets before loading them into the tray they can become stuck and jam the feeding points. No-name paper is fine for low volume jobs or home printers, but it should never be used in expensive machines pushing out thousands of pages a day. Any short-term savings are illusory when you have to pay for a service call three times a week."

I knew the contract with the *Ricoh* reseller included a set number of service calls. But in the few months since the machine had been installed it seemed every other day a technician in a red *Ricoh* polo shirt was pulling apart the device and fixing it. The new girl explained that the instruction manual recommends brands and types of paper, but ultimately it was up to the users to decide.

"It's in *Ricoh*'s interests to send out technicians," she said, "because after a set number of visits they make a small fortune out of fixing machines which should never have needed it in the first place!"

After the drama with the *RMFD780*, I introduced Claire to the rest of the team. I could tell everyone was surprised someone new was starting. I called the service number and was told they'd have a technician there in half an hour. I thought that was pretty responsive. Claire had said *Ricoh's* after sales service was the best around.

I walked my new colleague to her workstation. She asked about my role. I explained how I supported the business development team by identifying prospects and generating sales leads. In short, I did the groundwork for our team members to make contacts, develop relationships, and position us to win business when opportunities arose. After we'd won the contract, our subject matter experts advised clients across a range of disciplines including accounting, strategy, functional realignment, business restructure, and financial analysis.

Claire wanted to know how business development was different to what she would be doing. I pointed out contract finalization was a specialist area, which came *after* business development. When we had a new client, the contracts team ensured all the details were finalized, service level agreements were in place, and payment arrangements were lined up with finance. I stepped out the differences by outlining how the role of business development was to identify where there might be market opportunities and how we might get our services out to market. On the other hand, the role of the contracts team was to make sure all the documentation was in place and legally binding.

Claire thought that made sense. However, interestingly, she suggested it might make sense to collapse the teams into one unit. I responded that, in practice, the teams work quite closely together. Having said that, I agreed there was room for better engagement, not just between business development and contracts but across the company generally. Greater collaboration was often talked about by senior management, but in a deadline-driven environment it was too easily put on the backburner.

I wished her luck and went back to the photocopier to check on my print job. The *Ricoh* representative was already there. He'd pulled the machine apart. I asked him why it broke down every few days. He said it wasn't a mechanical fault. Rather than it having anything to do with the paper jam Claire had sorted out earlier, it was a firmware problem.

I had a couple of reports to print for my manager and asked if the machine could be up and running in the next half hour. The technician said it wouldn't be a problem—everything that had been sent to the printer when it broke down would remain in the queue. I watched while he opened a laptop and patched it into the *RMFD780* through a USB port. The machine was downloading a new version of the firmware from the laptop, after which it would automatically reboot. After a few minutes, the update was complete and the printer restarted. As the technician had promised, my printing resumed. However, I'd printed single-sided color instead of double-sided black and white. While it didn't make any sense, I would have to reprint everything or there would be a complaint about costs.

The technician confirmed Claire's advice that we should be using better quality paper.

Not a great deal happened in the next few days and it wasn't because of the downturn. I'd finished a long week developing leads which I'd passed onto my boss and business development colleagues to chase up. While I wasn't the type to present to clients on our service offerings, I was recognized for being able to identify sales opportunities. By way of example, a new industry might have been established locally or become more mature over the last twelve months. Perhaps the business environment was such that there was increased pressure on an industry sector to adapt to economic drivers or a new regulatory environment, or to adopt new technologies.

It was my job to identify where there might be a call for professional advice and when it would be needed. I'd come to that part of the cycle when I'd done the research on the potential client base and now it was up to Steve, Bridget, Alan, and Jaime to make calls, set up meetings, and see if they could make deals. Although it wasn't as if I had nothing to do, things would quieten down for a week or so, at least until I received feedback on whether the leads would result in any contract negotiations.

I didn't see much of Claire. It wasn't surprising given she'd only just started. She'd be finding her feet, getting to know the business, and sorting out who was who. The next time I saw her was again in the photocopier room. She was binding contracts and sales reports. Claire was laughing triumphantly, holding up a ream of *Ricoh* branded paper like a trophy.

"Someone must have taken the initiative and ordered some high-quality paper," she almost shouted. "The printer's working like a dream!"

Claire said the real test was high volume printing. If the machine could handle multiple double-sided print jobs it was apparently a good sign. I explained my conversation with the technician of a few days ago about the firmware update and told her it was I who had asked the admin team for higher quality paper. Claire smiled and congratulated me on my business acumen. She asked if I'd like to join her and her boyfriend for a drink after work. Claire thought we'd all get on well. I asked Claire what her boyfriend did for a living. She said he was a filmmaker.

Claire and I left the office at 5.30pm. The bar I'd recommended, *Whiskey-a-go-go*, below street level on Castlereagh Street, was tiny. Unless you arrived early it could be quite uncomfortable. As Claire and I were walking along Pitt Street before turning right into Bathurst and left into

Castlereagh, I asked how she was settling in. Claire was happy to report everyone had been very supportive. On her second day, they'd bought her a birthday cake even though it wasn't her birthday for another six months. There must have been a mix up with the date on her application form. She was touched by the gesture but thought it best not to mention anything. I joked she could now enjoy two birthdays.

My new colleague talked about work. Her main responsibilities were making sure contract documentation was complete and service level agreements were realistic. She considered it more of a legal role because she had to double-check contract details and make sure it was as easy as possible for the client to sign on the dotted line. It seemed to her all the interesting work was in business development and demonstrating the company's products and services. However, like me, Claire couldn't imagine fronting up to a potential client and pitching in front of a PowerPoint presentation. Claire reached into her handbag, extracted a packet of tobacco, and expertly rolled a cigarette. She'd finished it by the time we got to *Whiskey-a-go-go*.

We went down a steep stairwell into a small, windowless space. Until a few years ago the bar had been a long abandoned underground storage area for a Manchester business. There were black and white photographs on the walls. One was of a husband and wife standing in front of the store in 1927. I think they were Egyptian or Turkish because the gentleman was wearing a fez. He had a prominent moustache. Perhaps they were Moroccan.

A waiter with a heavy orange beard, tattoos up to his chin, and a large ring through the middle of his nose showed us to a table. There was hardly anyone else there. Claire asked for a pinot gris and I ordered a bourbon. She was talking about the quality of the wine and how cool the bar was when a man of about Claire's age sat down at our table. It was Claire's boyfriend. I'd forgotten he was coming. He introduced himself and held out his hand—*I'm James.* He called out to the barman that he would have what I was having and asked how our days had been. Like his girlfriend, he had a way about him that immediately put me at ease. James said he'd heard a lot about me.

We exchanged a few pleasantries before I asked the energetic young man what sort of films he made. He didn't quite answer the question. He'd finished at the National Film School a couple of months ago, made dozens of short films, and even won a couple of minor prizes at European festivals. James hoped the small overseas successes might lead to something. While he was only just making ends meet through TV work and music videos, he felt he was heading in the right direction. James described the difficulty in getting experience on features, and particularly on *quality* films. He'd worked on a couple of American movies that had been made in Queensland. One of them was Spiderman IV. I said I hadn't seen it. James and Claire laughed.

Claire said it was just a typical stupid Hollywood action movie blockbuster. James had been a runner for the continuity team and didn't have anything to do with it creatively. James agreed, but noted that despite the movie not being his thing it was good to be on set and understand the mechanics of a large film project. He wanted to go to Europe and work with contemporary cutting-edge film directors. Claire was equally enthusiastic. She'd never been outside Australia. The thought of going to France, Germany, Italy, or even Russia appealed to her.

"It won't be easy," he said, "but you must give these things a go. I'm not the type to die wondering!"

When we were about to leave, Claire revealed James had written a screenplay for a feature film. I asked what it was about. Claire looked at her boyfriend, put her hand on his, and suggested he let me read it. James looked slightly embarrassed, perhaps considering whether he should share his work with a relative stranger. I wrote my email address on a coaster.

When I arrived home, I reflected on the evening. I felt fortunate to have met two young, intelligent, and engaging people. Although I wasn't up to speed with all the modern artists, filmmakers, and musicians they talked about, I knew enough to feel included. And it wasn't just obscure artists James had referred to as his influences. He mentioned cinematic legends like Pasolini, Antonioni, Truffaut, Kulrich, Bresson, Lang, De Sica, and Fellini. I'd heard of most of them but was only familiar with Fellini.

At *Whiskey-a-go-go* I told them I once had a girlfriend who owned a Fellini DVD box set and that my favorite was La Strada. James agreed it was an excellent film. He didn't think it was fully realized but I didn't understand what he meant. I thought it eerie and melancholic, but also strangely amusing. After being exposed to their enthusiasm for art and life, and how they were taking chances, the idea of returning to work and developing business leads was underwhelming. I knew theirs was a life beyond me, and too late for me to explore. The last time I'd tried something out of the ordinary, it had turned into a nightmare, one that still haunts me.

I turned on the computer in my bedroom to find I had twenty-seven new emails. One was from a James McNeil. I almost deleted it before I realized it was James, the young filmmaker. As promised, he'd sent me the screenplay. There was a short note—I hope you enjoy *The Secret Writer*, Regards, James. I sent it to print but decided to read it when I was fresh and could give it my full attention.

⋆

The next day my team leader, Steve, came over to my

workstation. He thanked me for identifying clients who were perfect for pitching to. As a result of my efforts, he'd had promising conversations with a number of *potentials*. Steve said things were definitely going to pick up and I deserved a lot of credit. I appreciated the recognition. While I didn't need the approval of people like Steve, who was one-dimensional and addicted to work, it made me feel good to get positive feedback. In practice, the company had an ad hoc approach to staff development and recognition, but a corporate priority was to build a culture of continuous improvement. I think that's why Steve was making such a big effort in front of the team.

Steve, Bridget, Alan, and Jamie were now busy following up leads, so my next priority was to prepare the regular report for the monthly executive meeting. The executive team was a group of senior directors who each reported to the state Executive Director, who himself directly reported to the national CEO. It was a special occasion when the CEO visited us. He'd walk around the office and ask what we were working on. There'd be muffins and cakes. He had a positive impact on the team but we didn't see a great deal of him.

Anyway, the monthly report outlined the link between business development and sales. It was how the company kept track of our sales strategy at the state level. The report wasn't difficult to generate, and I'd done many before, but it was time-consuming. A key part of the work was to liaise with Claire's team to get data on contract arrangements and their dollar value. There were often add-ons I needed to factor in to ensure management had full visibility of outgoings and margins.

I went to see Claire on the east end of the floor. When I explained what I needed and for what purpose, she immediately pulled up a spreadsheet that contained everything—financial data, contract value, and who had initiated the sales. It was going to turn two weeks of work into just a few days of compiling information and generating charts. I told Claire her spreadsheet was going to save me a great deal of time.

"I knew the data would come in handy," she said, "and that it should all be in the one location. It was just a question of collecting it as it came to hand and copying it across. Everything was there already, just in different places!"

I offered to buy her and James a drink by way of thank you. Claire laughed me off saying James had nothing to do with it, but we nevertheless arranged to meet at a wine bar across the road from the office. Claire said James was keen to get my feedback on the script. I confessed I hadn't read it but promised to after we caught up. I was disappointed when Claire postponed the catch up until I'd done my homework.

We arranged to meet the following evening. Before going back to her desk Claire said I shouldn't thank her for the sales data she'd helped me with. She was just doing her job.

★

I felt a little let down. I'd been looking forward to catching up with them. There was something magical and other-worldly about these confident young people who were keen on making the most of their lives. They had a real plan for their futures. James' was to make films with high artistic standards, while Claire wanted to see and experience the world. They made a good couple and I hoped they'd be successful.

I went home to read James' work. I would order some takeaway, pour myself a glass of wine, and immerse myself in the script.

Picking up the document from my Canon Inkjet printer, the title page read:

*The Secret Writer*

*An original screenplay by James McNeil*

My heart rate quickened. My chest tightened. I questioned whether I'd be able to provide meaningful advice. I would be honest, but at the same time didn't want to risk my relationship with either of my new friends. I wrestled with these immature concerns for some minutes before plucking up the courage to read my first screenplay.

I flicked open to an early scene set in London. The characters were Karl Marx, the German philosopher, and his personal assistant, Viktoria Asarov. It was three o'clock in the morning. Marx's study was poorly lit. He was pacing up and down, talking, and correcting himself. The philosopher was dictating *Das Kapital*, a book I'd heard of but never read. Marx spoke urgently, as described in the direction preceding the dialogue. He was frustrated at his inability to get his ideas down on paper as quickly as he would have liked. Meanwhile, his assistant was infinitely patient. She hardly said a word. Unfortunately, after just half of the scene, the rest of the pages were blank. My printer had run out of toner. I didn't understand why it hadn't just stopped printing and thought about buying a more up to date model.

I arrived at the office at seven the next morning having emailed the script to my work address. Keen to get through the entire piece in one sitting, I logged on and printed it to the *RMFD780*. Although it was against office rules, I chose single-sided. It's easier to read a long document in that format, especially when you've bound it and put it in a folder.

When I went into the printer room I had a moment of panic. The *Ricoh* was shaking from side to side—something I hadn't witnessed before. I was concerned my personal printing was going to jam the machine and embarrass me in front of the rest of the floor. Everyone turned a blind eye to a page or two of personal material. But a four hundred and seventeen-page screenplay would have been frowned upon, especially if it resulted in another service call.

I needn't have worried. The unfamiliar sound was the printer starting up from offline mode. It was a relief when James' story came out without a paper-jam or need for a firmware update. By the time I'd hole-punched and bound the document, it was only seven twenty-five. It would be a good hour before anyone else arrived. I went downstairs, walked across the road to the food court, and ordered a coffee. I reflected on a man of James' age writing a story about Karl Marx. Marx was famous for the *Communist Manifesto* and *Das Kapital,* but apart from that I knew little about him. It seemed an unusual choice of subject matter.

However, as I soon realized, Marx's ideology was peripheral to the story. He *was* a major character in the screenplay, along with his wife Jenny von Westphalen and great friend Friedrich Engels. But the whole setup was only a vehicle for the story of Viktoria Asarov who, in addition to being an expert personal assistant and note-taker, was a novelist. Even though her fiction would have changed literature forever, Marx ensured her work never saw the light of day.

I couldn't put the screenplay down. It had a physical impact on me. As I had already experienced that morning while waiting for the printer to start up, my heartbeat increased. I broke out in a heavy sweat when reading the more dramatic sequences. There were moments of exaltation and pure terror. I

Apart from the narrative, which was remarkable and overwhelming in its detail, the screenplay (noting I'd never read one) seemed expertly constructed. James had included guidance for each scene—where the actors would be standing and a brief outline of the characters' states of mind. He described how each scene would transition to the next. It was a language developed specifically for screenwriting but it was easy enough to follow. James referenced the sounds that would accompany the action. He made no mention of music, but there were annotations to indicate, for example, a clock was ticking, birds were singing, or a door was being slammed.

I was taken aback by the complex chronology. The film started at the *end* of the story with a fire tearing through a nineteenth-century London boarding house. The fire ignited when a candle was knocked over by a woman's hand. The woman was Viktoria Asarov. There was shouting on the streets and general panic. I could hear old-fashioned fire engines being hauled by horses and bells ringing to clear the roads. It was clear any action would be too late. Flames had engulfed the building. The firemen, with their antiquated equipment, could only stand and watch in despair.

Then, suddenly, I was pulled back in time to the scene I'd started the previous evening. Marx was dictating, his secretary taking notes, the great thinker pacing around the room in an agitated, impatient state. She was taking down what was to become *Das Kapital,* the hugely influential book that changed economic and social theory forever.

*The Secret Writer* was without doubt the most incredible story I'd ever read. Although I'm not often moved by fiction, there were tears in my eyes as I read the last page.

It wasn't a conventional narrative. It was more intelligent than a straightforward story that starts at the beginning and finishes at the end. Of course it's not exactly groundbreaking to start a film in this way. I'd seen several that had used a similar conceit such as *Pulp Fiction* and *American Beauty*. But the story was more than that. It *interwove* narratives and timeframes. There was no present in *The Secret Writer*. There was also no future. Initially, I was confused by the constant movement between these impossible dimensions. There were dream sequences that seemed incredibly true to life until it became clear, through later developments, they couldn't possibly have been part of the 'real' action.

Viktoria Asarov is a young woman living and working in Saint Petersburg. She finds some early essays by Karl Marx. The essays are radical for the time. She has also read Marx's fiction and is enthralled by it. A colleague of Viktoria's, at the library where she works, has been able to obtain the texts through underground contacts who share their Romani ancestry, a detail they must keep secret at all costs. Those with Gypsy blood have been ostracised, imprisoned, and murdered across Europe for centuries. Russia is no different and the authorities are scapegoating anyone they suspect of mixed race.

Viktoria is the result of a brief encounter between a traveling minstrel violinist father and her mother, a St Petersburg orthodox Russian Christian. Thankfully, Viktoria has inherited her mother's fair features allowing her to dissolve into the mainstream Russian lower-middle class. Living in a city characterized by extreme poverty and fantastic wealth, and understanding the plight of the working classes and those persecuted for no reason other than their ethnicity or poverty, Viktoria sympathizes with Marx's ideas and resolves to work with him. She makes the arduous journey to London to find the great man and convince him to employ her as his assistant.

Asarov is an accomplished but unpublished writer of narrative fiction. She wants two things. Firstly, to work with Marx, assist with the development of his theories and see them make a difference. Secondly, she is confident her own work will find a sympathetic ear in the great man, who will help her find a publisher.

The young Russian librarian arrives in London after a journey of many weeks. She finds Marx's house where he lives with his wife and daughters and offers to be his secretary in return for somewhere to stay. Marx, impressed by Asarov's knowledge of his early work, consults his wife, Jenny, and his confidant and great friend and collaborator, Friedrich Engels. Marx relied on a healthy but irregular income from his writing and public appearances. He was by no means wealthy and reasoned that Asarov could assist him in being more productive. On that basis, initially for a trial subject to meeting Marx's exacting standards, Viktoria Asarov became the assistant to one of the most influential thinkers in history.

But it was Asarov who was central to everything. Her work was revolutionary. It was described, in the screenplay, as a pre-echo of Faulkner, Joyce, Marquez, and Hammett. Viktoria wrote furiously when time allowed. She tried desperately to convince Marx to provide an opinion of her work but never succeeded. The philosopher would always delay in order to keep Asarov close to him. He valued the way she refined his thinking and how she made his writing more logical, succinct, and precise. However, Marx was concerned that if she were to be published she would become successful, even more so than the great man himself, and he would lose her.

In this way, James built an unbearable tension between the mentor and his assistant. Asarov would ask Marx to read her work every few days, every few weeks, and then only rarely. Eventually, she was without hope that he would agree to her requests. No matter how miserable this made her, Asarov understood she was tied to him. She had no money and was reliant on Marx for room and board. A return to St Petersburg was impossible.

Another, equally significant part of the screenplay, was the plot of the Asarov literary masterpiece—the adventures of generations of German Gypsies and how they took on the legal establishment for their own financial benefit. The writing of this epic masterpiece was undertaken in the hours Asarov had to herself in her tiny room, sitting at a table in near darkness. Such was her devotion to her craft she hardly slept.

The final scene, replicating the first but in more detail, reveals Asarov in the midst of a fierce fire in a tiny London bedsit. Marx had died years before. His family had left her nothing. She lived off the generosity of Friedrich Engels who had given her a small annual stipend in gratitude for the services she had provided his friend. As she suffered a fatal heart attack, the candle fell onto a sheet of blotting paper that had been used that very evening as the unknown Russian writer put the finishing touches to her greatest work.

Asarov died alone and heartbroken. The thousands of pages she'd written, work that would have had a significant impact on generations of writers, would be read by no-one.

When I finished the screenplay I looked at my watch. It was 9.30. I'd been so engrossed, flicking backwards and forwards to double-check details, I'd finished it in less than two hours. I'd walked the streets of St Petersburg and London. I'd traveled in caravans through northern Germany in the company of a band of Gypsies. I'd heard the conversations. I could hardly wait to see Claire and James. I was interested to know if James had actors in mind. It occurred to me the precise nature of the direction would require performers of refined ability. But unfortunately I didn't see Claire that day. The contracts team was at an off-site business planning day.

When I got back to my computer I had ten new emails. One was from the Executive Director who wanted the report I had been working on brought forward to the following morning. There were people coming from interstate. It wouldn't be fair to describe his request as demanding, but he wanted the information as soon as possible. Ordinarily, producing the document to such a deadline would have meant working through the night to pull the data together from different sources, generate the charts, and then double check everything before going to print.

This time, because of Claire's foresight, most of the work had already been completed, conveniently located in the one spreadsheet. I had checked, printed, and bound ten copies by late afternoon. I handed them to the Executive Director, whose office was on the next floor. He was surprised I'd been able to complete the work so quickly. I explained how a new girl in the contracts team had helped me. He didn't know who I was talking about, but he was very grateful. It looked like a weight had been lifted from his shoulders.

When I got back to my workstation the phone was ringing. It was Claire asking if we were still on for that evening.

Claire and I arrived at the wine bar at almost the same time. She'd been dropped at the office after the offsite planning session. I asked her if she enjoyed it.

"Oh god, how I hate offsites," she said. "But at least they hired a professional facilitator to help get discussions going. I mean most of the time business planning is nothing more than an excuse to use up the training and development budget before the end of the financial year!"

At the offsite they'd mapped out, based on contract data over the last three years, likely activity for the next three, six, nine, and twelve-month horizons. She suggested I could have contributed to the outcomes, even only on how they could better support other teams. I remembered how she'd talked about the potential for more collaboration. I knew she was right about the need to get people working together where their work was complementary, or where you might want to run an idea by a colleague to get a different perspective. The problem was people felt comfortable in their silos.

Claire said she hadn't been *too* forward with her ideas. She'd only been with the company for a short time and didn't want to appear as if she was trying to take over and had all the answers. Anyway, by way of responding to my question, Claire said it was a positive experience—as long as the recommendations turned into practical outcomes. I told her not to hold her breath.

She asked how long I'd been with the company. I was a little embarrassed to say it was approaching ten years. After running a traveling show and a period of study, I'd started in administration and then moved into business development.

The reason I'd been with the firm so long was that I lacked a clear idea of where I should be headed. The conversation made me realize, if I needed any encouragement, I should be pushing myself and getting out of my *comfort zone*, a term people often used at work. Sometimes colleagues talked about the need to *stretch yourself.*

Claire was intrigued at the mention of the traveling show which was in fact a small-time circus. I was grateful James' arrival prevented me having to answer further questions. The young man was agitated and put his hand on Claire's. He looked from her to me and back again, tapping his foot anxiously on the floor, clearly nervous or excited. Perhaps something was terribly wrong. Claire noticed it too and said as much.

James said he'd explain later. He was desperately keen to know what I thought of the screenplay and terrified I wouldn't think it was any good. I told him I was no expert but in my view it was, without doubt, compelling in a way I'd never experienced fiction before. James put his hand on my shoulder and beamed at me. I noticed his perfect teeth as he asked what it was I liked most about *The Secret Writer.*

I spoke of my initial confusion at the multi-textured nature of the narrative. But I also pointed out that the complexity was counterbalanced by the richness of the characters and the interplay between them. The story became alive as I talked—Marx, Asarov, Engels, Jenny von Westphalen, Henry Gaurige, and his band of Gypsies—as if sitting right there with us.

"James," I continued, "the soundscape is so neatly rendered. I love the way the screenplay gives direction on what the audience will hear. It makes everything so real and so convincing. And the characters...they are so well drawn and, how can I put it, surprising. Strangely, the story is about none of them but all of them at the same time. It's about as *unhollywood* as you could get."

James laughed and clapped his hands.

"Nick, you are right," he said. "I'm so glad we agree on that point! It's exactly what I intended. While the story is grand in scope, its telling must be very low key. If not, the film will lack tension. You get it! You really get it."

James agreed with my description of the narrative resolutions but said he hadn't thought of the story in that way before. He asked me to comment on plot and structure and how they work together, or even against each other.

"Well of course both aspects are crucial," I said, "because they contribute to making the story both complex and evocative. But you can't really separate structure and narrative so neatly. If I were to say anything I suppose I'd say the concept is, in a strange way, about sublimating the characters in favor of an idea. Now I *know* I'm not making sense!"

Then I corrected myself. Something revelatory occurred to me.

"No," I said, "I think I may be right after all. It's not the characters...I mean they're important, but they're merely vehicles for the overarching conceit. I've only just this minute realized your story is about the *writing*. I'm not sure what I mean but do you understand? Ultimately, it didn't matter if the books were ever read by anyone other than the author. Viktoria's work foretold something about great literature of the future."

Claire was staring at me as if I'd arrived from another planet. She looked at her boyfriend.

"Nick's right," she said, "it's about the writing! I can't explain it but now I understand."

James was close to tears. He was visibly shaken by the conversation and the impact his screenplay had had on me.

Claire took the opportunity to ask James why he was so on edge. He came out with the remarkable news that an English producer liked the script and wanted to talk to him about it. Some weeks ago, James had caught up with one of his lecturers from the National Film School and given him the screenplay. He wasn't sure whether his former teacher would read it, but he had, he'd liked it, and without asking, had emailed it to a friend in London. The friend happened to be a young, successful film producer. James cited a few examples of the producer's work and although the names of the films were familiar, I had seen only one—*Another False Dawn*. It was a period movie about the end of the First World War. Jeremy Irons played a German army captain wrestling with desertion in the face of the horrors of the Somme.

I was excited for James and Claire who was looking adoringly at him. I could tell they were holding hands under the table. I offered to do anything I could to help. James was just grateful I'd taken the time to read the script and provide such insightful feedback. He told me my perspective had made him think differently about his own work. Although James said it was too soon to celebrate, I ordered a bottle of champagne I couldn't afford and waved away the young couple's protests. It was Veuve Clicquot. We toasted to the future. Despite the excitement, which James downplayed, he was interested in our work, business consultancy and sales, and how that world operated.

I explained my role, much as I had done for Claire on her first day. She said she was enjoying her job in contracts but thought there was a lot of room for organizational improvement. She couldn't believe such an old-fashioned culture could exist in the twenty-first century. James laughed and suggested that Claire and I should get out from behind our computers, become his business managers, and handle all the contract negotiations. I poured the last of the champagne and toasted to a million-dollar film deal. James even said he'd find a way to get me involved should the project amount to anything. Claire had a feeling that things were going to move quickly. While James protested it was just some early interest and nothing more, she suggested he should be careful to retain artistic control.

Claire reached across James, touched the middle finger on my left hand, and asked me about my ring. It was a Claddagh and many people asked about it. I said it was a long story that would keep for another day.

"The next time we go out," Claire said on seeing me in the printing room the next day, "we should do a Friday or Saturday and avoid the workplace hangover!"
I couldn't get James' script out of my head. We talked about Viktoria Asarov's great never-to-be-published novel, the masterpiece about a Romani family living in Germany told across three generations. The Gauriges traveled in garishly painted caravans. They took advantage of little-known legal loopholes to assume ownership of vacant land by occupying it for extended periods. One of the family's sons would assume the property title while the other Gauriges would move on to repeat the process elsewhere. It was an impossibly simple method of what amounted to legal theft.
The Gauriges built up considerable landholdings. The ever-traveling band of Gypsies became so rich and powerful the authorities were forced to reclaim the land by force. However by that time the family had sold much of what they owned. They continued to move across Europe, with vast quantities of money and jewellery hidden in their caravans. Curiously, their lives were untouched by wealth despite the lengths they had gone to acquire it.

I asked Claire how James had conceived of such a fantastic story. Perhaps he'd seen a documentary or read about Marx and his life in London. But there was surely no explanation for the story of the Gauriges and Viktoria Asarov. Claire had asked James the same question but had never received a proper answer because, she suspected, there wasn't one. While James was influenced by some of the great film directors (Tarkovsky was a particular favorite), he was also a fan of the Russian novelists Tolstoy and Dostoevsky. and wanted to make something similarly epic in scope. The young director was hoping for news in the next couple of days. She would be sure to let me know.

"Imagine if something happens! We could be going to London, and Germany, to make a movie!"

It seemed I, too, was now part of the project.

When I got back to my desk there was an email from the Executive Director. He wanted to see me. On occasion, he would call you up to his floor, but more often he would surprise you at your workstation. He would ask what you were working on or why he hadn't received a report he'd asked for. When I walked into his office I was surprised to see Claire was already there. She had her back to me sitting on one of two visitor chairs either side of a meeting table. The Executive Director wanted to tell us how impressed he was with the last set of business reporting and, in particular, how quickly we'd turned it around. Claire and I credited each other for the outcome. Then, without any warning, the Executive Director said he wanted us to work together on a special project. We would temporarily be seconded to a more complex business reporting assignment.

He explained the task while emphasizing we were free to approach the project in whatever way we saw fit, as long as we delivered the outcomes. We would collect financial and operational data from across the business with a view to making recommendations about how it could be run more efficiently. This would include an assessment of where process improvements could be made and costs could be reduced. We would engage closely with all units to gather the information and provide a holistic view of what was working and what wasn't. I, as the senior person and because I already knew everyone and had a deeper understanding of the business, would be the project lead.

"Listen," he said, "it's a big ask, but it will position you well for future opportunities. What do you think?"

Of course, we both agreed. It wasn't the sort of thing you could say no to. Besides, it was an opportunity to be recognized at the executive level. Claire couldn't believe she was being asked to step up so soon. I thought she deserved the opportunity. It was like I was listening to someone else when I said it showed what a difference a fresh set of eyes can bring to things. Later that morning the Executive Director sent an email to all staff, outlining what Claire and I would be doing and his expectation that everyone would contribute their ideas to making the firm a great place to work.

Over the following days Claire and I prepared for the project initiation phase. She suggested we sit down individually with each business unit to collect relevant information. I agreed. However, I also insisted on a project plan outlining the intended outcomes and key milestones. If we went to the teams with a clear idea of what we were doing and why, it would encourage our colleagues to work with us.

I explained how important it was that our job not be perceived as a report on, or a review of, the performance of other teams. In my view, we should present the task as a collegial one that would benefit all staff, much as the Executive Director had done in his staff email. Even this was risky, but I knew the personalities in the office and thought it the best approach. Claire hadn't considered how our work might be seen as a threat. We worked up the project plan while talking again about James' story. It was never far from our minds.

I explained how it had only just occurred to me that the idea of the Gauriges taking on established society was cleverly aligned with both Marx's socialist theories and Asarov's ethnicity. I remarked on the images that struck me the most—brightly painted caravans pulled by giant draught horses, children being born beside open fires, endless travel across the continent. I described how I heard music being played on home-made violins and the voices of children who never had to obey any rules. We talked about the prospect of James getting the project off the ground, but he'd heard nothing further from England.

By the end of the first few days of our reporting project, we'd developed an eight-week plan. We prepared a template for business units to fill in, or for us to complete, after our interviews. After this initial stage, we would send the information back to each team for review so they check for any inaccuracies. We thought it important that the teams had oversight of the process, so they would feel engaged in the outcomes.

We weren't just collecting quantitative data but qualitative information too. That was Claire's idea. She thought it would allow our colleagues to offer their own insights into their day to day work experiences, areas for process improvement, and to generally assist in encouraging them to be more open.

The office was buzzing with the news of the project. As expected, there was a certain disquiet around the place. Questions were being asked about Claire's suitability for the job. I'd been around for years, but she'd only recently come on board. I sensed people doubting her ability to get across the business in such a short period of time and being suspicious of a newcomer making recommendations that could affect their futures.

One morning in the kitchen, I interrupted a young man from admin and a woman from legal discussing whether Claire had only been hired because she knew someone. They were concerned the business development and contracts teams were losing resources when everyone was under a lot of pressure. Claire and I worked through that negativity. Relatively quickly we got to a point where teams would even come to *us* with information and their own ideas. I enjoyed having something different to do and the collegiality only made everything easier. It was a pleasure working with Claire, too. We saw things in the same way and if we disagreed about anything it was easy to resolve our differences. After only a few days I couldn't imagine going back to my normal role.

Even though we were busy arranging meetings and collecting information, we knew James had been exchanging emails with the English producer. While there was nothing concrete, James had been asked to prepare a storyboard so the producer could understand how *The Secret Writer* would be filmed. James had been working, sometimes through the night, on a PowerPoint presentation. It seemed I wasn't the only one with questions about the practicalities of turning such a complex narrative into a movie.

Claire suggested we go out for dinner so James could tell us where it was all up to. He'd been so busy, working through the day on his video work, and on *The Secret Writer* through the night, they'd barely seen each other. As she was asking about dinner, I noticed an anomaly in the financial data. It seemed some of the consulting work undertaken by my team had not been billed and allocated to the contracts unit. I pointed this out to Claire who agreed it was unusual. She said it may be just a time-lag issue.

On closer investigation, however, it became clear what the problem was. I'd been generating leads and they were followed up as normal. However, not all the contracts and sales data were going to Claire's team for finalization. Some of the business development team were dealing directly with clients and invoicing them, or taking cash payments, without anyone else in the business having visibility over their work. In short, it seemed certain individuals were doing private consulting, billing the clients themselves, and pocketing the money. If intentional it was clever, because the sums were not so large that anyone would notice.

Claire and I talked about what action we should take. There may be some justification for operating in that way. It was possible the executive team knew of the practice. But it didn't feel right. Sensibly, Claire suggested we find out more detail. We needed to be sure of the facts and agreed if we weren't careful we could put ourselves in an awkward situation. I suggested the gaps in the data could perhaps be explained by human error, but I didn't really believe what I was saying.

Claire pointed out we were not even three weeks into the

project and we already had all the data and qualitative information we needed. With my experience and her expert spreadsheet skills we could quickly complete the report, write it up and do the charts, and then relax for the next few weeks at least. Claire said we should finish the report on the weekend and effectively have a paid holiday! We laughed about, but were concerned by, how little the executive team knew about the business.

Claire convinced me we could use the time to plan for James' film. Her energy was contagious even though, as far as we knew, no film contract had been put on the table, let alone signed. We left work a little early to meet up with her young film director at the *Whiskey-a-go-go.*

I knew James must have good news when there was a bottle of Moët and three glasses waiting for us.

"These early inquiries," he said, "often come to nothing. But this producer, Elliot, against all odds is going to back us and finance the film! The producer has convinced a consortium of financiers (he didn't know who they were) to come up with many millions of pounds and (James was almost breathless at this point) had offered the script to a famous British actor who was interested in the role of Marx."

Claire and I both wanted desperately to know the name of the actor, but James had no more detail. We knew as much as he did. He was going to the UK in two days.

"The best part," James said, "and wait for it...is that you are both coming! I've arranged for 'my team' to join me!"

Claire was excited. I was more circumspect. I had no idea what I was getting myself into, and Claire and I had a significant work project to complete. I had no wish to put our current opportunity at risk. It might be ok for Claire, but I was in quite a different situation. If I could deliver the report with meaningful and practical recommendations, it might enable me to move into the executive stream. She seemed to know what I was thinking.

Claire convinced me that because the report was basically complete, we could argue we'd be able to finish it more quickly by working out of the office. I didn't want to spoil the atmosphere so I undertook to ask our Executive Director for approval to work from home. After all, the company had a flexible work policy I'd never taken advantage of. James understood my predicament but assured me I was needed in London. There may be pre-contract agreements to sort out and he would value my advice and experience. I didn't say anything, but Claire was in fact better placed to advise on such things.

It was hard to believe how quickly things were progressing. Claire and I had been identified for the special assignment at work, and now I was being taken to England to help out on an international film project. I was returning to the entertainment industry, albeit in very different circumstances.

I wondered if my life was about to take a turn for the better, or if I was dangerously moving into a world I knew nothing about, with two people I'd known for only a short time. For the second time in my life I decided to take a chance and put everything at risk.

The Executive Director didn't think twice about approving our leave.

The journey to the UK was largely uninteresting except for the fact we flew business class. Claire and I managed to almost finalize our draft report before we even arrived at Heathrow airport. We didn't mention the financial discrepancies in the document, instead resolving to raise them verbally if we couldn't find a reasonable explanation. We talked James through the dilemma and, while he was somewhat distracted by the excitement of going to London, he agreed we should be cautious about raising anything before we had all the facts. He made the point that people are innocent until proven guilty. James spent much of the journey annotating his screenplay and going through the storyboard on his computer. He asked us at one point, in a moment of understandable anxiety, whether the Asarov novel was perhaps too complex a concept for film. While I still had concerns about how the story might come to life, Claire and I, in different ways, thought the novel was the best thing about the story. Claire joked it might open up the possibility of a sequel—a standalone film about the Gauriges. Although it was a crazy idea, the same thing had occurred to me when I first read *The Secret Writer*.

When we got off the plane James received a text message from Elliot. He apologized for not being there to meet us but had sent a car to take us to our hotel. In the arrivals area a man in a black suit was waiting for us. He was holding a handwritten sign with James McNeil's name on it. We were welcomed and ushered into a limousine. The driver said Mr Elliot had another appointment but would meet us at our accommodation. I could tell James was nervous. The situation was becoming strangely real and he was silent on the journey into London. We arrived at our boutique hotel, where a young man in an immaculate, red waistcoat with gold buttons took us to our rooms.

I was sitting on the bed when my phone rang. It was Claire. Elliot had arrived. I found the three of them laughing about something. I was introduced as James' commercial adviser and shook hands with the producer. He was gregarious, friendly, and looked no older than thirty. Elliot had great news. He wanted to fast-track production and, incredibly, gave us the news that Daniel Day Lewis had signed on for the project at a vastly reduced fee. Day Lewis would take the lead role of Karl Marx.

Elliot's announcement about the famous English actor threw me. I panicked at the strangeness, the unfamiliarity, of the situation. I broke out in a sweat and felt rather ill. Should I pack my bags and head back to Sydney? I could return to the pedestrian life I somehow couldn't do without. Elliot's enthusiasm, however, brought me back to the moment. He explained that Day Lewis reads many scripts but accepts very few. *The Secret Writer* would be the first film he'd made since his academy award winning performance in *Lincoln*. I'd seen it some years ago. I didn't say I'd found that film a little wooden and far too long. I also didn't mention I thought the lead performance very impressive.

Elliot had other appointments. He left, but not before arranging a meeting the following day. He'd booked a restaurant for us for dinner. As soon as the producer disappeared, James sat down on the king-sized bed and put his head in his hands. He looked exhausted—as if it was all too much for him. Claire asked what was wrong. I felt like an outsider and started back to my room. James waved me back. "Please," he begged, "anyone but Daniel Day Lewis. I know what will happen. The film will become a biopic of Karl Marx and be promoted as such. Day Lewis will appear in every scene. We will lose Asarov and Engels. Engels is pivotal! The story of the Gauriges will become a mere subplot to the life of Marx. The story is not about him! It's not about anyone! It's about the book that was never read and the invisible writing that exists all around us. I would have had Fassbender, Cumberbatch, perhaps a German actor like Jurgen Prochnow—even Thomas Kretschmann. They are all actors who understand a script and how to respect it. You can see it in their eyes. I want," James said sadly, "magic not realism."

I protested Day Lewis was surely one of the finest actors, if not *the* finest, of his generation. Claire suggested Fassbender could take the role of Engels, or even the Gaurige patriarch. James looked around, shaking his head. He thought the project was turning into a mistake and he would have only limited control over production. *I wasn't even asked!* James implored me to carefully review his contract to ensure he retained a say in casting.

I was alerted to a new email on my phone. It was from the Executive Director. I excused myself and went back to my room.

✱

The Executive Director wanted an update on the report, and whether it was on track. There was a new intimacy to his communication. His note suggested the cyclical lull was not being well managed. The company, he wrote, needed to modernize and come to grips with new ways of working rather than just talking about it. I let him know he could have it the following week. I didn't tell him it would take no more than a few hours, and Claire and I could finish it that very day. As Claire had predicted, we would be able to enjoy our time in London and be back in Sydney with time to spare.

When I returned to their room, James was staring from the hotel window onto the street below. He snapped back to his normal, positive self.

"Seriously, who am I to complain? I have my film just about up and running and backed by one of the best in the business. I can talk to Daniel Day Lewis and explain my ideas. He's clearly intelligent and I know he can be reasoned with."

James admitted he shouldn't be making assumptions when he hadn't so much as met the actor. He asked Claire and me to excuse him for his ridiculous behavior. Even so, I could see the question of Karl Marx was playing on his mind. Changing the subject, Claire suggested we be tourists for a day and explore Islington, where our hotel was located. James and I readily agreed.

We wandered the back streets lined with narrow three and four storey Georgian houses which looked better suited for people half our size. We stopped every half hour or so at a pub. We made a pact not to talk about *The Secret Writer*, Daniel Day Lewis, or Elliot. Claire and I chatted about our own work and resolved to finish the report after dinner. James asked if there was anything he could do to help. I appreciated him asking and said he was welcome to provide feedback if he wanted to. I joked it wasn't really in the same style as his screenplay and that it lacked the same degree of narrative complexity.

James' worries seemed to have evaporated. He received a call from reception telling him our car was ready to take us to the restaurant. A message from Elliot informed us we should order whatever we wanted. We laughed at the situation we found ourselves in. It was hard to believe the situation had any firm basis in reality. I asked the chauffeur for the name of the restaurant. He said we were going to *L'Arpege* in Paris. The three of us looked at each other before quickly retrieving our passports from our hotel rooms.

On the way to Paris, Claire found the menu on the restaurant website. She laughed loudly when she called out the prices.

"If we were paying," she said, "a couple of main courses would cost us two weeks' wages!"

After a drive of a few hours we arrived in the center of Paris on the Rue de Varenne, right outside the restaurant. We were shown to a corner table and asked for a menu in English. Sensibly, James asked for the chef's recommendations with matching wines. The portions were tiny but delicious. We ate fish, duck, beef, artichokes, truffles, beetroot sorbet, and many other specialities. The food was a little unlike food. You might say it was more decoration than sustenance. We shared three bottles of wine—a vintage Krug, an aged Chablis and an Haut-Medoc cabernet. The service was excellent. Every time we even thought about asking for something, a waiter would appear having anticipated our request.

Inevitably, in spite of our earlier agreement, the three of us started discussing *The Secret Writer*. James canvassed potential locations, suggesting the North London Georgian terraces would be perfect for Marx's home. They were neither too grand nor too humble. For the Gypsy sequences, James wanted to shoot in Germany. Interestingly, he seemed to be softening his views about the cast. James accepted that at this early stage of his career he shouldn't be too precious about all the key decisions.

I offered that a man of Elliot's stature wouldn't take on a project unless he firmly believed in it, and he was hardly going to make risky choices. I wanted to emphasize that James should trust the producer while remaining firm it was *his* film and *his* story. Claire, more drunk than either of us, laughed at the fact that while James was wrestling with the casting and producing a multi-million dollar film with one of the biggest names in the industry, she and I still had a business report to finalize.

She almost shouted, banging her fist on the table, that the first thing she'd recommend would be for the company to invest in new technology and printers. Or, better still, that the firm bite the bullet, go fully digital, and do away with paper altogether to get costs down and enable collaboration. We all saw the funny side of the stark differences between our respective challenges.

Claire gestured to the waiter for another bottle of Krug. As she did so, none other than Daniel Day Lewis walked into the restaurant. He came over to our table and introduced himself to James, Claire, and me.

Day Lewis was both shorter and taller than I'd expected. For some reason I had the promotional poster of *The Last of the Mohicans* in my mind. I thought he'd look wilder and more menacing, but his hair was cut short and he looked quite unlike his character in that film. After all, it was some twenty years later. The actor wore a t-shirt and jeans, the only exceptional thing about him being his maroon caterpillar boots which made his feet look enormous. After we'd shaken hands and identified James as the director, the actor talked enthusiastically about the screenplay. He had an unusual accent. I couldn't tell whether it was English, Irish, or American.

Day Lewis apologized for interrupting our evening, but he *desperately* wanted to meet us. He spoke softly and urgently, like he was sharing a dark secret, about the importance of making high quality films based on great stories. For someone of his considerable achievements, he came across as a man of great humility. He was careful to include all of us in the conversation.

Day Lewis turned to James while clicking his fingers. Almost immediately a large bottle of Perrier appeared before him.

"Why," he asked, "did you write about Karl Marx?"

James didn't move a muscle, but I could see the tension building inside him. He looked about to explode. After a pause that almost certainly went unnoticed, he responded that the story was not in fact about Marx, but rather, if it was about anyone at all, Viktoria Asarov was the central character.

"While Marx is of course pivotal," he explained, "the story is about Asarov's secret writing. Or," he said, while glancing in my direction, "the film is about all the stories in the world that remain untold but nevertheless exist all around us."

Day Lewis looked pensive, as if considering James' comments, and proposed a toast to the project and, in particular, to the director, Mr James McNeil. The great actor's presence was intoxicating, but I could sense that it had caused some awkwardness, at least on the part of James. It seemed James' fear that the movie star might derail his vision could be realized.

Despite what James might have been thinking, I found Day Lewis totally engaging. He was comfortable revealing a little about his family. His father had been poet laureate, and his grandfather the head of Ealing Studios—a famous English film production company. He was ageless and could have been thirty or sixty. The actor was generous to a fault, picking up the bill and waving away our protests.

Day Lewis' parting words outside the restaurant were *There will be blood!* We all laughed even though I had no idea what he meant.

As we drove through the channel tunnel, James discussed acting and performing, trying to explain the difference.

"The prevailing view of acting is a tedious one," he said. "It developed in America in the 1930s when Stanislawski took his method acting theory to New York. In broad terms, *method* is about the actor *becoming* the character. The actor's persona completely disappears. The actor as actor ceases to be, and instead is replaced by the character."

James corrected himself and said *replaced* was the wrong word. "No," he said firmly, "the actor as a vehicle for the character would *evaporate.* If successful, the audience will suspend its belief and see the spectacle as real. Of course, we have all been to the theatre or cinema and experienced moments when we forget ourselves and become immersed in the action. But this is only a transitory sensation. In my view it's impossible to achieve for the duration of the performance in the way that Stanislawski, among others, envisioned. The problem is the actors can lose the writing and the sense of it—they replace it with a characterization. In this way they also lose respect for the author. This is what Diderot foresaw two hundred years ago. Everything is lost! Actors become so self-absorbed in their own actions, movements, and vocalizations that the script—the text—becomes secondary to the *craft* of acting. The actors should be a vehicle for the text, not the expressors of it, and yes, I know this doesn't make sense!"

I didn't admit that I'd never been to the theatre. To be honest, I didn't follow James' logic at all. However, I gathered he wanted his beautifully crafted narrative about the secret Russian writer and her generations of Gauriges in all their Romani glory to be the features of his film, not the actors. I knew nothing about the subject, but it seemed to me there should be a more balanced way of thinking about it because without the actors, there would be no performance.

We were close to the hotel. My mind turned to the report from which Claire and I had been distracted by Elliot, high-end French cuisine, and our meeting with Daniel Day Lewis. Putting James' obvious concerns about the actor to one side, I liked him. He was down to earth and interesting. In addition to some interesting anecdotes about his family, he told us about his plan to build a replica medieval sailing boat he would take across the Irish Sea.

✶

I woke early and reviewed the report on my computer. For the first time there was a clear picture of how the business was operating and where there was room for improvement. I could not only see where there were opportunities for better collaboration and information sharing across the teams, but also where they could be brought together because their roles were so complementary. And, importantly, more details emerged of where, it seemed, payments were being made directly to two senior members of our team—Steve and Jaime. While Claire and I had been suspicious, there was now no doubt embezzlement was occurring, and on a grander scale than we'd previously thought. Put simply, some contracts were not being finalized in the normal manner. Examining the raw data from the last two years I could see deals worth many thousands had never made it to Claire's team for contract finalization. It was a simple deception, and difficult to discover, because the individual amounts were not substantial. The only reason it came to light was because, for the first time, we were reconciling information from across the organization. There had never been such a comprehensive audit of the business at the micro level.

I wanted to give Claire a final draft in hard copy so I called reception to ask if someone could print it for me. I went downstairs with the file on a USB stick, and the clerk sent it to print. However, some minutes after waiting for him to hand me three copies, he emerged with the news the printer was jammed. He would have to make a service call. I asked him for the model. It was a *Ricoh RMFD780.* I smiled at the coincidence and assured him my friend would be able to fix the problem. We chatted for a few minutes about the unreliability of printers and how much they cost to maintain. The man at the desk said *they can send a man to the moon but they can't make a printer that works nine times out of ten!* When I returned to my room there was a note under my door. Claire wanted to know if I would meet her for breakfast at a café not far from the hotel. She wanted to talk about the report and our return home. I walked out into a bright, crisp London morning.

I met Claire at a café across from the Angel underground. The café had an Italian theme. There were black-and-white photographs of Vespa motor scooters, Sophia Loren, and Italian village laneways. There were reproduction prints of Pellegrini soft drink advertisements. One of the photographs was of a tiny street, almost completely empty except for washing stretched between the balconies of neighbouring houses. The face of a small Italian boy peered out from one of the windows, directly at the camera. It was a beautiful, nostalgic image.

Claire was sitting at a corner table reading a newspaper. She looked up and asked if the report could be finished that morning. She didn't want to think about it anymore. I said I had a final draft, but because of the printer issue she'd have to review it on the computer. She laughed when I explained the situation with the *RMFD780*, but immediately became more serious when I revealed the significance of the financial irregularities. Claire knew it could be awkward for me given I'd been at the firm for such a long time and worked with the people involved. She pointed out that if the business was run properly, issues like this would have been picked up sooner. Claire picked up her coffee and talked about the previous evening. It occurred to her James was right. She shared his fear that a big-name actor may turn the project from a carefully nuanced and textured narrative, to one concentrated on a single characterization. She now understood how a focus on performance *per se* would bury the text, and even dissolve it, which was one of the words James had used on the ride home. I argued against this, noting Day Lewis was an intelligent, thoughtful person who chose his film projects carefully. I was hopeful James and he could work together. I thought, and I said this, Daniel was clever enough to realize the script was an opportunity to do something different with his career. "Anyway," I offered, "it's hardly a disastrous situation."

On our return to the hotel the fellow at reception showed us the photocopier. The red lights were still flashing. With considerable dexterity Claire opened the machine, pulled some levers, and removed the blockage by turning a handle and extracting some ten or so sheets of torn paper. The machine came to life and, after the few minutes it took to restart, the report printed out in full color, single sided, and stapled. I was relieved it wasn't a firmware problem.

Claire sat in the foyer on an oversized arm chair and read through the document. She pointed out typographical errors and said it needed an executive summary. She thought it unlikely the report would be read in its entirety and, if it was, it would only be because the summary pointed them to the most important parts. There were two overarching themes that needed emphasizing. Firstly, in her view, the financial irregularities had to be carefully positioned so we weren't making any specific allegations. Secondly, she wanted to highlight the recommendations about realigning business units into a far more streamlined structure with fewer teams and clear accountabilities.

For some reason, I wanted James' opinion. I thought his level-headed approach and independent perspective would be of value. I also wanted to run it by Daniel Day Lewis. It was a crazy idea of course and when I mentioned it to Claire she threw her head back and laughed.

"You can't do that," she laughed. "However you'd have to admit that it's a great story with all the makings of a serious drama! Of course, Day Lewis would have to play the lead role!"

I agreed and said he'd be perfect as our Executive Director.

Claire disagreed. She thought Day Lewis would have to play me because I was the one on whom everything turned.

"By the way," she asked, picking up my hand, "when are you going to tell me about that Claddagh ring?"

I didn't like to talk about the ring, but it was an unusual piece of jewellery. Not many men would wear such a thing, but it was of great sentimental value. Colleagues would ask where I got it and whether I had an Irish background. Claire looked at me closely and suggested someone special must have given it to me. I explained I'd been given the ring by a performer I'd been involved with during my circus days. It was long before I'd come to the city.

"You see, Claire," I said, "work was hard to come by in the country. Where I lived, it hadn't rained in ten years. The place was a dust bowl and wasting away. Most young people moved to larger towns, or Sydney, as soon as they could. It was a rather unusual set of circumstances that resulted in me running a circus to make ends meet. I knew nothing about the arts."

Claire asked where the circus was now and what had happened to the woman who'd given me the Claddagh. I explained how, some months after having abandoned my job, a fire had destroyed everything. It had been one of the acrobats, Tama, who had given me the ring. We'd been planning some sort of future together but I'd not heard from her again.

Claire looked into my eyes like she was seeing me for the first time.

✳

Elliot arrived at the hotel later that morning. He could hardly contain his excitement. Apparently, Day Lewis had been impressed with us at our dinner in Paris and was keen to start casting and pre-production as soon as possible. The actor shared Elliot's concerns about whether the right people would be available. Elliot wondered aloud who might play Marx's friend and confidant, Friedrich Engels, because it was such a pivotal role.

"A German actor would be ideal," he suggested, "however, unfortunately, the best candidates are involved in other projects. On the one hand, we could delay until casting was finalized. On the other hand, I must say I'm keen to press on, get moving, and take advantage of the finance on offer. Day Lewis is already half way through *Das Kapital* and has enrolled at the University of London to study Marxist theory and German. I wouldn't be surprised if Dan spoke only German for the next six months!"

James pointed out the screenplay was almost entirely in English and that the only German was spoken by the Gauriges. Elliot smiled, a little patronisingly I thought, and said that was beside the point. Dan would need to get inside Marx, immerse himself in the character, and take on every part of his psyche.

"Anyway, my young director," Elliot asked, "what, ideally, would *Engels* look like? Who is he exactly? He's a bit of a mystery both historically and in the script. Marx gets all the credit but my understanding is Engels was just as influential." James described Engels as middle aged, about five foot six, and of slim build. As was the custom in the mid to late nineteenth century he wore a heavy beard. Engels was quiet and unassuming. While he didn't have the same desire for fame or notoriety as Marx, he could still take significant credit for a completely new way of thinking about society, class structure, and economics. Engels was Marx's right hand man. Without his support, he would never have reached the heights of one of the great intellectuals of the last two hundred years.

Elliot looked at me with a disquieting intensity. He asked how long James had known me because it seemed that except for the beard it was me whom he had just described.

I assumed Elliot was having a joke at my expense. However, it soon became clear that the idea of me as Engels resonated with James. He looked me up and down while holding his chin in his hand.

"You know, Nick," he said, "it's not such a mad idea. A few weeks ago we were sitting in a bar in Sydney with this crazy ambition to make a movie. Already we've met one of the most important film producers in the world, not to mention Daniel Day Lewis—and we are in London planning for production! Having a mysterious new actor whom no-one has heard of could be just the ingredient the film needs. You could be the difference between success and failure. Heavyweight casts are all very well but they can have a negative impact on the film's believability."

I answered that the fact I'd never acted made me the least likely candidate for such an important role. He disagreed in the strongest terms and countered that some of the finest films had been made with untrained actors and a number of the best directors relied on them.

"Think about Rossellini's neorealism," he said, "or even Mike Leigh and Ken Loach as examples of English directors who see the value in using untrained performers. Pasolini was another who relied on novice actors and improvisation. This is not to say their films were not carefully designed to account for such uncertainties."

Claire asked me what I had to lose and reminded me, somewhat embarrassingly, how I'd been in the same job for years.

"I suspect," she said, "you're desperate for change but unable to. How could you possibly say no to a screen test? You might become rich and famous! You'll never need to think about that fucking report again!"

As it happened I didn't want to be famous, and I *did* want to finish the report. However, no doubt because of the circumstances I found myself in, I heard myself saying I'd help out if I could. As soon as I'd put the finishing touches to the document and given it to our Executive Director in Sydney, I would consider an audition. Elliot walked over to me, put his hands on my shoulders, and told me I *must* test for the role. The success of the film might rely on me. Daniel had told him I was a straight-ahead thinker. I had no idea what that might mean in terms of being able to act, or why Day Lewis thought it necessary to comment about me in such a way.

I wanted to get back to Sydney. I told the group I was going to my room to adjust the report based on Claire's feedback. Before I'd shut the door behind me, I heard Elliot say *what report?* Claire said it wasn't worth explaining.

The day before our return to Sydney, I emailed the final draft to our Executive Director. Just thirty minutes later he replied. Claire and I were to present the findings to the executive team on the Monday of our return to work. Claire offered to prepare PowerPoint slides. She suggested I come over to her place on Sunday so we could run through the presentation. Claire hoped this would be the last office work she would ever do.

James didn't come to Heathrow to say goodbye. He was meeting a script editor that morning. The project was going ahead and at great speed. Even having met Day Lewis, I continued to have doubts a film project of this scale by a young Australian director would ever get off the ground. The screenplay was impossibly complex, with so many layers, so much movement between dimensions, that it would be terribly difficult for a mainstream audience. It occurred to me, while accepting I was a novice, that the story might be better suited to a novel where the reader has the luxury of being able to reread and consider the complexity at their leisure.

The flight to Sydney was uneventful. We had a brief layover in Singapore before the final leg of the journey. We didn't talk much and neither of us mentioned James, his film, the famous people we had met, or the company report we had co-authored. Claire bought Absolut vodka and Issey Miyake perfume at the duty-free shop at Sydney airport.

I'd never been to Claire and James' suburban Leichhardt apartment but found it easily enough after a twenty-minute bus ride from the city. Claire opened the door and welcomed me with a dramatic wave of her hand—as if I were walking into a mansion. The walls were covered in movie posters. There were two faux Academy Award statuettes that served as bookends. Camera equipment was lying around on the floor. The place was a mess but bohemian and interesting.

Claire opened her laptop and took me through the presentation. I was impressed by its thoroughness and clarity, and grateful she was seeing the process through to the end. The only suggestion I made, and which she agreed to, was to have two extra slides. The first would provide a high-level overview of why the report had been commissioned. The second would provide contextual information about current operations with a chart depicting interactions and dependencies between the various business units. It was a question of providing the problem statement before going into detail on potential operational changes.

Claire wanted me to do most of the talking. Even though we both now understood the complexity of the business better than anyone, she would only step in where necessary to provide what she still considered to be an external perspective. I was happy Claire was keen to know what the reaction to our recommendations would be. Now we were back in Sydney, it seemed Claire had refocused on bringing our work to a successful conclusion.

After we'd finalized plans for the next day, she kissed me on the cheek and said *break a leg!*

The next morning I was nervous, but felt well prepared. It was comforting that Claire would be there as back-up. The Executive Director met us as planned. He was impressed with the thoroughness of our work. While he broadly agreed with the recommendations on business realignment, he was concerned about the financial irregularities in the business development team. I was relieved we'd been able to brief him separately. It was important he was across the detail before any executive level discussions took place.

Claire and I were called into the boardroom at ten thirty. We were the only item on the executive team agenda. There were twelve people seated around a long, oval table, in the middle of which sat a large plate of muffins and savoury slices. The muffins had been cut into quarters. The executive team had iPads and glasses of water. Our presentation was loaded up on their machines. All of them were men with the exception of one woman about my age. She was the only person I hadn't seen before. The Executive Director introduced her as the new Chief Operating Officer. She had a strong background in people, culture, and performance. The COO took off her glasses, thanked the Executive Director for the introduction, and said our report was both sensible and concerning.

Even before Claire and I had a chance to speak to the PowerPoint slides, she said the recommendations should be implemented as a priority, and staff from the business development team should be placed on immediate, unpaid leave until a proper investigation could take place. I took the group through the report and answered questions. Claire answered those about the more complex financial details. Then it was all over.

It was satisfying to have completed the project. Of course, this was only the first step before the implementation phase, during which there would be wholesale changes to the business model. It wasn't lost on me that people were going to lose their jobs, but I couldn't see any alternative. There would have to be redundancies because there was, as we had clearly identified, considerable overlap between the teams.

Claire and I knew streamlining the operational and consultancy areas would mean, in effect, fewer people doing the same amount of work but working more efficiently and collaboratively. We also talked about what the changes might mean for us. Claire was confident, given we'd done the hard work identifying where to drive change, we would never be let go.

"Anyway," she said, "we don't need to worry. I'll be a production assistant on James' movie, and you'll be an international film star!"

We were sipping coffee when the Executive Director called. The executive team had agreed to full implementation and a thorough investigation of the financials. He asked us both to take at least two weeks off. An inquiry into the alleged embezzlement would start immediately. He didn't want either of us to be in a position where we might be targeted. I didn't think that would happen because at no time in the information gathering phase did we give any hint we were suspicious of anything. However, I agreed there was potential for recriminations.

Claire was excited. She wanted to return to London immediately and meet up with James. She reminded me, with a mischievous look in her eye, about my promise to audition for the part of Friedrich Engels.

"A great many actors have been discovered by chance," she said. "Kirk Douglas and Johnny Depp are just two examples. There's no reason you can't be one. It's not so difficult. You just learn the lines and pretend to be someone else!"

In a moment of weakness, no doubt buoyed by the success of the presentation, I had let down my guard and said I'd take the test. Straight away, Claire was on the phone to James who, apparently, already had in mind the excerpt he wanted me to read. I could hear James' excitement. He would talk to Elliot in the morning and make arrangements. I would be reading one of the longer Engels pieces.

James asked Claire to give me the phone. He reminded me of a long conversation between Marx and Engels, a particularly moving part of the screenplay, where the latter was arguing about Asarov and her place in Marx's life. I remembered it well. Engels reveals his concern about the relationship between Marx and Asarov, and the potential damage to the great man's family, reputation, and fortune if there were rumours of infidelity.

"Remember," James said, "Engels never found out about the secret writing!"

It was good to take time off work and not just to avoid

potential repercussions from adverse staff reactions to the report recommendations. I found myself with nothing much to do and enjoyed waking up with a free day ahead of me. Claire and I stayed in touch. We'd become close. I felt the friendship keenly when I told her about the email from Elliot's production company about the screen test. It was to be held at a Sydney film studio. Claire took the audition far more seriously than I did. She insisted on visiting me on each of the four days before the reading.

I was nervous the first time Claire knocked on my door. Not because I felt uncomfortable around her, but because my place was not particularly welcoming. Claire and James had movie posters, books, and records littered all over their small apartment. I owned nothing even remotely as interesting. Although I'd lived there for years, it seemed there was no personal dimension apart from a relic of my former life—a *Circus Mundo* poster Claire found interesting for its *art deco* style. She found it terrifying but didn't say why.

I printed off two copies of the Engels speech to my Canon, one each for me and Claire. I'd bought two new toner cartridges. Like a director, Claire reminded me Engels was pleading with Marx to let go of Asarov, or at least work with her more discreetly. Claire reminded me I needed to inhabit the nineteenth century. She wanted me to bring a subtle formality to the reading while also remembering Marx and Engels were close friends.

I read the piece from beginning to end, trying my best to be

Friedrich Engels. Claire's only recommendation was to learn the piece by heart. She said I was a natural.

I recalled the discussions with James about acting. By the time I'd read about half the piece, I became lost in the moment. That is, I forgot myself and became, as I understood it, a vehicle for the text. James' thinking resonated with me. I was beginning to understand the difference between acting and performing. No doubt the following description of my experience will seem ridiculous, magical, or perhaps even crazily religious. Nonetheless, at some point during the reading, the text became three dimensional. It rose from the page and circled above me, waiting for me to become a part of it. Then, incredibly, the words chose me and became me—or I became them.

I thought I'd momentarily become Engels, but I realized the absurdity of that idea. I could no sooner become Engels than he could become me. Even if you were to describe the transition in that way, the only Engels I could become would be the artistic approximation James had created in his screenplay. Perhaps I disappeared and became James' writing. But I couldn't be sure on that point either. Most likely I'd forgotten myself, which is hardly an unusual occurrence for anyone.

After reflecting on Claire's feedback I realized I had, in fact, given into or surrendered to the text. The writing made the acting easier. The sentences were short and well constructed. The dialogue was formal yet evocative. It carried the voice of the rigid nineteenth century yet was full of raw emotion.

I was interested in, and enjoyed, what had happened to me. There was a feeling of personal release I'd never experienced before. I resolved to put a good deal of effort into the screen test. I took Claire's advice and learned the passage by heart. After three or four readings, I could recite the piece without a mistake. I recorded myself and listened to my voice. On the evening before the audition, Claire came to hear me practice for the last time.

I'd been thinking more about what had happened to me during those rehearsals. If anything, by the time of my last reading to Claire, I realized how I was increasingly disengaged from myself during each performance. I became someone else while not being sure who, or what, I had become. Nevertheless, I hovered above my body, observing myself in operation. I was neither myself, but nor was I Engels. I had become something that existed between me, James' characterization, and the writing.

I found the experience liberating. It was like a sleight of hand carried out by god while I was sleeping.

We were greeted at reception by a woman with a tattoo

of a blue dolphin on her left wrist. She led us to the studio where I would do my screen test. The production assistants and cameraman were helpful and efficient. One of them pushed me gently into position. She pointed to the camera and explained they would do the test from two angles. In the first, I should stand at a forty-five-degree angle to the lens but not look at it. In the second I would be looking directly at the camera while pretending the lens was Karl Marx.

The test passed quickly. I had no idea whether the readings were good, bad, or indifferent, but Claire kissed me on the cheek and said she felt quietly confident. Consistent with my own feelings, Claire thought I'd become the character in a way she'd never witnessed before, as if I'd left the room to be replaced by someone else. Claire used the word *transformational*. She asked if I were real and pinched me on the arm.

"Am I imagining all this?" she asked. "Am I really working with Nick Clement in a boring old office and on a major international film project?!"

I agreed with Claire's description of my audition. I explained to her the exquisite feeling of having ceased to exist, and how that sensation became more acute with every performance. It seemed I'd learned to lose myself—to disappear. In spite of my misgivings, I confessed I enjoyed the experience very much. That evening, James called from London. He and Elliot had reviewed the footage and were enthusiastic. Elliot had apparently joked about actors doing all that training when someone like me could do it without thinking! James also commented on, and laughed about, my *disappearance* during the reading.

"Nick," he said, "it's a part of you I'd never have guessed existed, or didn't exist, whichever way you think about it. You were not the person I know so where in hell did you disappear to? Are you Nick Clement? I honestly don't know...but at least you're Friedrich Engels, and that's the main thing right now!"

Elliot demanded I go back to London immediately so we could start pre-production and read-throughs. James was happy to confirm Elliot was employing Claire as his production assistant.

I was excited about going away again, however, there was the small matter of taking leave for an extended period. I felt I was letting the side down by authoring the report and leaving others to implement it. When I caught up with Claire, I asked whether she would permanently leave the company. She couldn't believe I was asking such a question. Claire said we should hand in our resignations and never look back. She admitted, however, that even in London, meeting the rich and famous, she hadn't felt as if it were real.

"Did we really have dinner with Daniel Day Lewis and his giant boots?" she asked. "I feel I'm going to wake up at any moment. In spite of all we've been through, there is a part of me that expects to find myself sitting at the computer writing another bloody report on business operations."

I decided to make an appointment with our Executive Director. I needed to let him know I'd be away for some time. Claire said she'd come too, but she didn't want to tell him about the movie. She thought he'd react badly to the idea of doing something creative.

That night I dreamt of James' Romani Gaurige family. I woke in a Gypsy caravan. There was an overwhelming smell of rotting meat. An enormous old woman, dressed in a headscarf and floral apron, was standing at a wooden bench cutting a large leg of stinking, red flesh into pieces. One of her breasts, stretching to her waist, had escaped from her blouse and was swaying from side to side.

She picked up the meat and tossed it into a black pot hanging over an open fire. There were thick floral rugs piled on top of each other. The woman asked me something in a language I couldn't understand, but I was aware she was asking me to eat. She poured a red powder into the pot, and the caravan filled with the delicious aroma of hot paprika. An old man, her husband, joined me at the table. We ate and said nothing. The woman continued to speak in her harsh, angular language. Her husband ignored her and ate with an ugly voraciousness. The thick casserole was spicy and delicious.

After I thanked her (now able to speak her language), the old man and I went outside. He told me, as a Gaurige, it was time I encamped on a property and acquired it permanently. He pointed to an old castle. It was in ruins and long since abandoned. He ordered me to live in it for seven years. I was to take my wife and children and not see him again until my mission was complete. The old man was now Marx. My wife appeared, and she was Viktoria Asarov.

I climbed into a caravan with my family. We went to live in the derelict castle. I can't remember whether I was happy or unhappy in the dream. When I woke, I thought of the three interwoven narratives—of Marx and Asarov, of the secret novel, and of the Gauriges, one of whom I had become. I hadn't underestimated James' gift for storytelling. His multi-dimensional narrative, with its separate but interdependent components, had entered my unconscious life. I was keen to know who he would cast as the patriarch of the Gaurige family who, in Asarov's great novel, recounted the history of the family over the generations.

Claire's early morning phone call interrupted these thoughts. She told me we'd be flying to London in a few days.

The Executive Director joined us at the food court café. Claire said she was resigning to take up an opportunity overseas. The Executive Director understood how Claire, as a young woman, would want to explore the world. He generously remarked that not many people can come into an organization and make such an immediate and significant contribution. Claire thanked him.

Although it wasn't strictly a lie, it felt like one when I told him I needed to go away for personal reasons. I would need six months or so but would remain contactable if he would be good enough to grant me leave. The Executive Director looked at us as if we were planning something romantic together.

"Nick," he said, "it's up to you, but there's an opportunity to step into a bigger role. The new Chief Operating Officer wants you on her team *going forward*. In fact, she wants *you* to oversee implementation of the new operating model."

I was tempted to step up into a position with more responsibility, but I politely declined while offering to be a sounding board if needed. I knew the outcomes might be more easily achieved if I had as little as possible to do with the restructure and suggested it might be better for someone to come in with a new perspective. Having said that, I knew the company realignment wouldn't be operationally difficult. The main obstacle would be legacy attitudes to new ways of working.

"I appreciate your honesty," the Executive Director answered, "but I must say I will miss you. Getting to know you through this project has been rewarding and, although it might sound strange, revelatory."

I was surprised at the comment because we had never, even on the operational review, worked closely together. I would have described our relationship as business-like rather than genuinely collaborative.

Claire and I went out for dinner the night before our flight to London. She chose an outdoor table at an upmarket restaurant close to the water at Barangaroo. When I arrived, she was already seated, drinking white wine, and smoking a hand-rolled cigarette. She stood up and kissed me on the cheek. I could smell port-soaked tobacco. I asked about her new role as production assistant, what she would be doing, and who she would report to.

Claire would report directly to Elliot and be responsible for anything from administration to paying bills and location coordination. Elliot had a number of projects at various stages of completion and she'd be working on all of them to some degree. Claire would be his representative and manage logistics. If, for example, more money was required for any reason, it would be her responsibility to either approve the budget increase if it were within a certain threshold, or advise him as to whether she thought the increase justified.

"In a way," Claire pointed out, "I'll be the conduit between the director and the producer, or a general dogsbody who does whatever she's told!"

I commented on the similarities between her new and former roles.

"I agree," Claire said, "but we should stop talking about work and start planning for an exciting future. You are far too calm and collected, my friend. How can I get you out of that shell? Are all actors enigmas, or is it just you, Nick?"

I didn't feel calm at all. I felt uncomfortable about leaving work at such a critical time, and nervous about the prospect of working with so many new people. I'd met Elliot, who was charming and energetic, and the intelligent and experienced Daniel Day Lewis, but there would be hundreds of others. It occurred to me that people who work in the entertainment industry would all be interesting in one way or another. Actors need to take risks and have a strong creative side to their personalities to make a successful career. I admired people who were able to shy away from certainty and reliability.

Perhaps, despite my ultimately disastrous period as circus impresario, I could succeed in the entertainment industry.

Claire and I met at the airport. On this occasion, she bought Balenciaga perfume. I bought a pair of Bang and Olufsen headphones which to this day I have never opened. As we walked onto the aircraft, the attendant looked at our boarding passes and advised we would be traveling first class.

We were met in London by a woman in chauffeur's uniform

holding a sign with my name on it. Nick Clement. Claire laughed. She said I had a good name for an actor. Our driver took us, not to a hotel in the city as I'd expected, but to an apartment outside London, near Pinewood studios. The apartment was one of four in an old manor house—*Pinewood Manor*. Claire, James, and I were sharing a large, three-bedroom suite. On the grounds were a swimming pool and gymnasium.

We were informed by the concierge there was a chef on site twenty-four hours a day, and we should avail ourselves of the service whenever we wanted. While it may seem indulgent to be able to order food at any time of day or night, it struck me that making a movie was hardly a nine to five occupation and it may be necessary to eat at unusual times. From the first class travel to our accommodation, everything had been organized to make our lives as comfortable as possible.

Claire said James would join us that evening. He was in London working on some minor edits to the screenplay. Remembering his sensitivity about the writing, I asked Claire if James was worried about changes to the script. Claire relayed what James had told her. The edits were merely a re-ordering of some of the scenes. The script editor had suggested the changes to make the narrative clearer.

Of course, reading a screenplay and watching a film are quite different things. When I first read *The Secret Writer* I had, on numerous occasions, flicked back and forward to make sure I was following the story correctly. While it worked on the page when you had the luxury of double-checking details, and it was interesting to seek out the narrative thread, it might not necessarily translate to film quite so neatly.

A mobile phone started ringing on the coffee table. Claire indicated I should answer it even though the phone wasn't mine. Elliot's name was displayed on the screen. I answered it. Elliot was business-like. He said to be ready at six o'clock in the morning for the first read through. A car would pick me up and take me to the studio. He and Daniel Day Lewis had spent the last few days extricating Kate Winslet and Tilda Swinton from other commitments. They would be joining the cast as Viktoria Asarov and Jenny von Westphalen respectively. *Wasn't that fantastic news?!*

I knew Kate Winslet from *Titanic* and *Revolutionary Road*. I'd seen the latter on DVD and very much enjoyed it. I had no idea who Tilda Swinton was.

James came home late, excited to see us. He'd met some great people and learned so much in just a few short weeks, hardly believing he was in charge of the whole operation. Whether it was costume, set design, special effects, or editing—Elliot had assured him he'd have final say over all creative aspects.

Elliot apparently wanted to spend some time with me, alone, to prepare me for what would be an entirely new experience.

He wanted to talk not just about the production side of things, but contractual arrangements, how much I'd get paid, residuals, and those sorts of things. The young director put his hands on my shoulders.

"How incredible will it be to act alongside Kate Winslet and Tilda Swinton? You'll never know what we had to go through to get them on board, but most of the credit must go to Elliot and Day Lewis for signing them up. They will be perfect!"

Claire pointed out, a little sadly, we might not be able to socialize much over the next few months. At least initially, her time would be spent variously at Pinewood, in the London production office, and in Germany, where she would scout potential locations. Elliot had asked her to explore options for the Gaurige scenes. She would assess whether it would be cost-effective to shoot overseas or whether a comparable outcome could be achieved at Pinewood. Claire said there are pluses and minuses for either option.

She thought, ideally, the Gaurige shoot should be undertaken in Germany where much of the action was set. Local technicians could be used or, at a cost, the production team could be flown over. However, if the same result could be achieved in England, and James was happy with the location, then she would look for nearby sites that would perfectly render a convincing Gypsy atmosphere. Claire said her Excel skills were going to come in handy for all the costing work she would have to do.

I wished them good night when it was clear they wanted to be alone.

I woke early, nervous about how the day would unfold. I wasn't concerned, I don't think, about acting. My fear, or unease, related more to the prospect of working with famous people in a completely new work environment. I would need to quickly adapt to the personalities around me.

It was still dark when my new phone rang. It was Elliot. He was outside in the car. When I climbed into the back seat the producer smiled warmly, apologizing for being ten minutes early. He told me again how happy he was I'd auditioned. I think he was trying to give me confidence for my first day. Elliot advised that while the casting had been a last-minute affair, both he and James couldn't be happier with the outcome. He would have liked to have told me about Kate and Tilda earlier, but didn't want to say anything until the details were confirmed. Apparently it wasn't unusual for actors to find out very late in the piece who they will be working with. Sometimes, he explained, the cast can even change after production has started.

Responding to what he obviously perceived as a lack of self-assuredness on my part (and I admit I was suffering from a particularly acute nervousness that day) I was advised to be myself and remember it was a unanimous decision to cast me.

Kate, Tilda, and Dan, I was informed, were generous people, and they were all looking forward to working with a new face. Elliot handed me an envelope and asked me to open it. Inside was my contract. He confessed that he had been remiss in not sorting out arrangements earlier. However, he noted, *The Secret Writer* was like a snowball rolling down a mountain. The momentum and size of the project kept increasing.

Elliot didn't get out of the car at Pinewood, where a security guard opened the door for me. As I was being led away to the studio, Elliot leaned out the car window and, in a final message of good luck, promised I was in good hands.

"But," he called out, "be careful around Tilda Swinton. Tilda can be prickly—she's the best actor around, but she's got a temper!"

As I was about to go through the door to Rehearsal Studio A, I was shocked when a man leaped across my path and pulled me into a corner. He was about sixty, a little overweight, with long, rangy grey hair, and a heavy beard. The stranger was wearing an old-fashioned three-piece suit. A fob chain dropped from a tiny pocket. This enigmatic gentleman was from another century. Either that or he was completely mad. He whispered in my ear. I could feel his whiskers against the side of my face. "It's Daniel," he said. "Daniel Day Lewis." I could hardly believe my eyes. Only a few weeks ago he looked lean and fit. He was now transformed into a man from another time and completely unrecognizable. Daniel was, of course, Karl Marx. He welcomed me to my first film project and wanted me to understand, from this moment on and for the duration of the production, he wouldn't be able to interact with me as he would when he wasn't working.

He was in a hurry and spoke rather breathlessly, but nevertheless took a few minutes to explain his approach to method acting. Daniel would become his character totally. He would *be* Karl Marx. If he was rude or difficult at any time, I was not to blame him but instead remember that I was dealing with Marx, not Daniel. The character before me (Daniel or Marx I couldn't be quite sure) asked that I respect the artistic process and his approach to characterization. Anyway, Daniel assured me there would be plenty of time to catch up after we'd finished production. He told me to break a leg, just as Claire had done before our presentation to the Executive. And with that he walked purposefully into the studio, a copy of the screenplay in his right hand. I followed, after catching my breath and steeling myself for what was to come.

Inside the large rehearsal room, four people were sitting on chairs set out in a circle. There were no cameras or film production equipment. I walked toward the chair with my name on it. Kate Winslet stood up, smiled, and offered me her hand. She graciously welcomed me to the entertainment industry. James rose and put his arms around me in a generous show of affection. Daniel was going over the script, muttering to himself in German.

A woman with red hair raised her eyes and looked at me briefly, perhaps dismissively—Tilda Swinton. I recognized her from the advertising for *The Lion, the Witch and the Wardrobe*, a movie based on the children's novel by C. S. Lewis.

Swinton looked like a ghost. Her skin seemed transparent and she was astonishingly beautiful. Without introducing herself to me as Kate had, Swinton made a sudden and brief announcement. She said while the screenplay was a long way towards being a masterpiece, we still needed to work closely together, especially given the director and one of the principals (she cast a quick glance in my direction) were so inexperienced. Daniel Day Lewis and Kate Winslet seemed indifferent to her comments. The former was still flicking through the script, the latter smiled at me as if to say *don't pay any attention*.

James took control of proceedings. I could hardly believe he presented so confidently to such a high calibre group. He'd never been short of self-belief, but he appeared composed and sure of himself in a way I hadn't seen before.

"Fellow artists," he said, "this is a significant occasion. It's the first read-through of my first feature length screenplay. I have spoken to all of you individually about my views on the characters and how they should be portrayed. That said, I am always open to discussion and suggestions. However, as I've made clear, I will not be making any changes to the dialogue." After the briefest pause, James continued...

"The central character is, of course, Viktoria Asarov (James looked to Kate Winslet) who, for reasons of intellectual curiosity and admiration for one of the world's greatest thinkers, travels to London with the ambition of working for and with Karl Marx. The first scene, which is really the final scene, returns us to the present after a fire tragically destroys poor Viktoria and her work. So, for this reading, Viktoria has arrived in London, desperate and hungry, all the way from St Petersburg. She wants to work with Marx, share her ideas about literature, and seek his views on her own writing. Viktoria Asarov is a woman who won't be denied but ends up *forever* denied by a cruel genius."

And with that, the first reading began. I had only a few lines at the end of the first domestic scene, when Engels arrives at Marx's home and his advice is sought as to whether the great man should let Asarov stay. Engels quickly establishes she is well-qualified for the position (she is educated and has some familiarity with socialist theory) and advises Marx he will be far more productive with an assistant.

The reading progressed well. Daniel Day Lewis, Kate Winslet, and Tilda Swinton were, I thought, very polished. It was clear they had already done a considerable amount of individual work before this first rehearsal. Daniel's German accent was entirely convincing. Kate's Russian pronunciation was equally formidable. Tilda's Teutonic lilt was slight but effective. Her

Jenny von Westphalen had the air of a woman who is desperately in love but who lives with an overwhelming sense of worry—as if terrified that at any moment something will go catastrophically wrong.

After the reading, when everyone had congratulated each other on a job well done (with the exception of Daniel who exited the room without saying anything), Tilda asked if I would have lunch with her.

The Pinewood studios cafeteria was surprisingly basic. It reminded me of a restaurant you might find in a factory. There were other projects underway in the large studio complex and I saw several actors whose faces I recognized from television or the cinema. People turned their heads in Tilda's direction as she walked by. I couldn't blame them. I was in awe of her transparent presence. She looked like she might fade into the ether at any moment—or breathe fire at you.

Despite the rudimentary cafeteria fitout, the food looked delicious. Tilda chose a light salad with vegetables which she hardly touched. I ordered fettucini carbonara. It turned out to be more of a creamy boscaiola, but I didn't mention anything. While my initial impressions of Tilda Swinton, who I soon learned had been a prominent figure in the film industry for over twenty-five years, led me to believe she was cold and distant, I quickly warmed to her. She opened up after the formality and hard work of our first acting session.

Tilda asked about my background. I told her a little about my erstwhile job and, surprisingly, she was intrigued by the mechanics of business consultancy. In particular, she was interested in the report Claire and I had just finished. She insisted I describe it in detail, and then asked about next steps and potential staff reactions. I told her the business realignment, although long overdue, couldn't be argued against. The bigger issue, which on reflection I should never have raised, was the question of corporate theft.

Tilda understood why I was relieved to be away from the business for an extended period and suggested a new acting career had come about at the perfect time. Interestingly, as Claire and I had once half-heartedly discussed, Tilda thought the story of the report and financial issues could be written up as a screenplay. She couldn't believe Claire hadn't mentioned this part of her life. In Claire's defence, I responded, she surely assumed, as I would have, that office work and business practices wouldn't be of much interest to someone in the film industry. Tilda countered that the film industry is also a business, and anything is interesting if you tell it in the right way.

"For example," she argued, "take any movie by Godard, Fellini, or Pasolini. The narratives alone, without the genius of the directors, could have been mind-numbingly dull. And your report would seem to have all the hallmarks of a great and modern melodrama. Anyway, people in entertainment can be dull too, and I include myself in that regard! Take Daniel Day Lewis for example. He's good, but like the rest of us he's made a career out of dressing up."

Before rehearsal recommenced, Kate Winslet was kind enough to say I'd done better than expected in the morning session. Although she was positive about my performance, she suggested I try and project a little more. I was grateful for the feedback and during the afternoon tried to speak louder and more forcefully. Day Lewis was holding the screenplay in one hand and in the other a copy of *The Communist Manifesto,* the book Asarov was assisting him with. He looked strangely absent, as if he wasn't with us. He was quite transformed, both physically and emotionally, from the man I'd met in Paris.

Shortly after we'd taken our seats, another woman came into the room. She was introduced as Hedwig, a voice coach, who would be assisting us with our accents. She'd been listening to the read-through from an adjoining studio. While Daniel, Kate, and Tilda's accents sounded authentic enough to me, I thought I could benefit from professional help.

Hedwig started with the Germans, which meant Karl Marx, Jenny von Westphalen, and Engels. According to her, while I didn't seem to be attempting a Prussian or German accent, I would only need to make minor changes to get the right result. She commented that my speaking voice was unusually accentless, which I took neither as a compliment nor a criticism. Hedwig explained how a simple but convincing German accent could be achieved by concentrating on enunciating from the back of the throat while keeping the consonants as short as possible. She emphasized the need to produce sound from deep in the chest. Hedwig asked each of me, Daniel, and Tilda to say one of our lines.

Daniel's accent was perfect, and Hedwig confirmed this by shaking her head and laughing in disbelief. After Tilda and I had spoken, she repeated our lines back to us but with a greater emphasis on the individual syllables of each word and what I discerned to be not only an emphasis on voice production from the back of the throat but from the top of the mouth as well.

Thankfully Hedwig was much more impressed with our second attempts. She promised that after a few days of thinking clearly about which part of the chest and mouth the sound was coming from, we would quickly get to the point where we wouldn't even have to think about it. The advice she gave to Kate Winslet about her Russian accent was equally interesting. She asked Kate to imagine the words being created in the back of the throat, as for German, but that they were being pushed from the mouth and around the tongue like a gentle breeze. Kate took the advice and used it immediately to create a voice that sounded like it came from the streets of St Petersburg.

✦

The rest of the day proceeded on schedule. We didn't stick to the scene order in the screenplay but moved things around according to James' instructions. Once or twice, I thought I caught him doubting some of Daniel's nervous ticks, or the facial expressions he used to signal Marx's frustrations. There was nothing definitive, but I sensed an impatience with the performance.

Working with Daniel was a somewhat unnerving experience because unlike Kate Winslet and Tilda Swinton, he never for one moment stepped outside his character. Even when asking for clarification from James on how he wanted him to approach a line, he would use his accent, or even ask in German before translating. By the end of a long day, which I found tiring even though we'd hardly moved from our chairs, we'd covered most of the Marx-Asarov London sections of the screenplay.

Cars had been arranged to take us back to our accommodation. While waiting for our drivers, Kate Winslet confessed to me she'd been slightly concerned at the prospect of working with someone without any experience, but she no longer had any doubts.

"I was so worried about your nerves," Kate said. "This morning I thought you might have been blown away by a gust of wind. But any concerns I had have vanished. You are now *taking on* the performance. I can hear you project. That audition tape wasn't lying!"

Kate and Tilda were going to London for a Giorgio Armani charity fundraiser. Kate asked if I'd like to go, but I declined. I wanted to rest and, in any case, I had nothing to wear to such an event. As Kate, Tilda, and I were leaving separately in our cars, I saw a horse and carriage coming along the driveway. It stopped in the waiting area as Daniel Day Lewis emerged from the studio dressed in his three-piece tweed suit. He climbed inside. I wondered what other extraordinary things he could do to ensure he remained in character. Perhaps he would write a manifesto of his own. I would never underestimate his total commitment to the characterization. It was incredible to witness his dissolution into character. Wherever he was going, it would have taken ages in the horse-drawn carriage. It moved barely at walking pace.

Claire was already at the apartment when I got there. She ordered hamburgers and handed me a Stella Artois. While waiting for dinner I checked my email. There was a note from my Executive Director. The subject line said *Update!*

It was a long email. Firstly, he hoped I was having a good time, whatever it was I was doing. The rest of the message brought me up to speed on the change process and the identification of those in the business development team who were responsible for the corporate theft. As it turned out, it hadn't been necessary to get a forensic analysis of the accounts. Steve and Jaime had put their hands up as those responsible. I was surprised. They'd always seemed switched on and professional. As Claire and I had suspected, they'd won the engagements on behalf of the business, and there were records of this because of my work as the business researcher, but they'd undertaken the consultancy work on their own and organized payments to separate accounts. The value of the theft was over one hundred and twenty thousand dollars but spread over so many years it hadn't been noticed. The Executive Director noted the illegal operation could have, and no doubt would have, continued for years without our review.

The first measure to be taken, consistent with what Claire had identified as an opportunity in her first days on the job, was to merge the business development and contracts teams. This would result in staff losses, but it was the most logical first step, and easiest to put in place, because Steve and Jaime had been stood down. Importantly, and again in line with our recommendations, the firm was recruiting a manager for the combined unit. They were looking for someone with business development *and* contract management and execution skills. The Executive Director was concerned it might not be easy to find someone with that skillset.

The second major reform would be a central, dedicated reporting unit to undertake quarterly operational reviews, based on input from all business areas. The unit would then report directly into the executive team. There would be a fortnightly high-level reporting dashboard to track performance. Claire and I had conceived of a rolling model where the business units would take turns with such a task. But I could see it would be optimal to have a dedicated and independent resource to maximise team engagement and ensure financial irregularities of the sort Claire and I had uncovered could never happen again.

Finally, the Executive Director mentioned that Japanese investors were interested in the firm and all this work would add considerable value to the transaction, if it went ahead.

I replied, thanking him for keeping me in the loop and saying I looked forward to further updates. Claire showed little interest. She was leaning out the window smoking a cigarette. She blew a smoke ring that only dissolved when it hit a stand of fir trees on the other side of the swimming pool.

On James' return he asked how I thought the day went. In my view, the talent at his disposal was going to make *The Secret Writer* a very successful movie. I told him how surprised I was at how well he was able to manage the considerable forces in the room. I doubted whether the first reading could have gone any better. James wasn't so sure. He was holding something back as he commented on the different approaches. "Nick, you must have noticed how Kate and Tilda tackle their work. It's almost unbelievable to watch. They can switch between themselves and their characters instantly. It's extraordinary! One moment you are observing a young, desperate Russian Gypsy who is trying to find herself in the world while looking for inspiration and guidance from the man she wants as her mentor. The next you are talking to Kate Winslet, an actor and mother with things on her mind that are totally unrelated to the film. You will have noticed Tilda. It's hard to take your eyes off her! There's an unusual stillness about her. I think, and I could be wrong, she uses this stillness to channel all her energy into the moment—that moment being Jenny von Westphalen-Marx. But again, just like Kate, Tilda can bring herself back instantly, as if nothing had happened. They can manage their epic but subtle transformations like no-one else. I forget who they are and find myself shocked when they re-emerge. You can see how they respect the text and understand their role in voicing it."

James asked me what I thought of Daniel Day Lewis' approach.

"Well, his total immersion in Karl Marx is somehow not acting, or perhaps it's acting in its purest form. It's not just the character that Daniel is taking on, but the late nineteenth century, the German language and even modes of travel. It's as if a journey in a car would be too distracting."

James and Claire laughed at my joke. James explained how Daniel was an exponent of the *method*, based on the work of Stanislavski, and later Adler, Meisner, and Strasberg. I knew of Lee Strasberg because I'd seen a documentary about him on

Netflix. He'd been a key influence on the acting profession, particularly in America, and had taught some of the giants of the industry including Pacino, de Niro, the Fondas, Dustin Hoffman, and even James Dean. The young director obviously knew a great deal about this way of working. He went on to outline how the *method* was a rigorous internalization of the character, rather than the traditional focus on adding external elements to the self to build the persona.

I understood this to mean actors would use their own experiences to create the character and then *become* or *live* the person they were playing. I asked whether this meant it was no longer acting but something else altogether. He thought it a relevant question and undertook to think about it further. The discussion came to a close when James said *method* was, despite what anyone said, a valid form of theatrical representation with by far the most currency in the industry.

Claire chimed in and said she was a *huge* fan of both Kate and Tilda. She named two of Swinton's films as her favorites of all time (*Orlando* and *I am Love*). James agreed they were great movies, characterized by expert storytelling and performances of overwhelming refinement. He hoped *The Secret Writer* might be half as good.

He revealed, however, that casting for the characters in Asarov's novel, the Romani Gypsies, was not going well. Elliot was working hard with the casting director on identifying, hopefully, German actors for the key roles. They were proving difficult to pin down for the filming schedule. In any case,

Elliot apparently had concerns about their suitability for an English production. I didn't understand what Elliot might have meant. There was, I thought, a definite international flavor to the production.

Contrary to Elliot's views, in order to create a completely different feel for the Gaurige part of the film, James said he was keen to use German, German-Swiss, or Austrian actors. Although I suspected James would disagree, I suggested the Gypsy scenes, which made up a considerable proportion of the screenplay, could easily be set in England, or indeed any part of Europe. In this way, I suggested, you could cast local actors who would be better placed to meet the schedule. Claire had initially thought the same thing but asked me to consider the position of the writer of the novel. She reminded me that the German angle was crucial because, although Russian, Asarov had deliberately set much of the action in and around Prussia, hoping the work would resonate with her hero, Marx.

"That's exactly the issue," James said. "We need to make it as authentically German as possible, irrespective of whether we film on location or not."

It turned out that Claire had been busy researching locations, visiting three potential sites that day, each being just outside Hamburg. She thought all three would be perfect for the exterior shots, both from an organizational, logistics perspective, and because the fall forests would provide a wonderful setting. However, she cautioned that the costs would be considerable because temporary accommodation would have to be built, and all the equipment would have to be hired and transported from Hamburg. In her assessment, based on initial calculations and against her better judgment, it would be cheaper to build sets at Pinewood and find comparable locations nearby. She would spend the next two days looking around the immediate vicinity of the studios, where there were wooded areas that might be a good fit. Suddenly, James stood up with a smile spread across his face.

"Hang on, let's get back to casting. I think I can see a way around the battle for suitable European actors. It's a compromise, but perhaps it's a much better solution than we'd ever imagined...the Gauriges and their story are a part of Asarov's imagination, are they not?"

Claire and I nodded.

"Then why," asked James in a moment of inspiration, "can't Daniel Day Lewis, Tilda Swinton, and Nick Clement also play the roles of the Gypsies? Surely Asarov would have imagined them as she was writing her novel."

An idea of such brilliance could have only come from the writer himself.

After a time of reflection, pacing around the room, Claire agreed it was an exceptionally clever idea.

"I think," she said enthusiastically, "it gives us more flexibility with the shoot. On a purely financial basis it will save us hundreds of thousands of pounds, if not millions. It will also mean we don't need to stick so closely to the notion of German-Gypsy authenticity. I love the idea of a small ensemble cast that can work closely together over the full production."

James disagreed with Claire on one point. He wanted to challenge the cast by keeping Asarov's novel authentically German. His view was if the production were to be *presented* as Viktoria's imagination, it would lose focus and become, as he put it, some sort of vaudeville.

"No," he continued while thinking aloud, "we use the same cast, but we also need to make the novel real. We owe it to Asarov to ensure the Gauriges come to life! This will fulfil one of the original intentions of the movie. That is, not to have any particular emphasis on either the real *or* imagined, and to keep the duality of the narrative in sharp focus. One thing is for sure—this is going to test the actors. I think we can do it. It will just require some serious thinking about character and further re-ordering of the scenes."

Claire thought we should run the idea past Daniel, Kate, and Tilda. She pointed out their contracts stipulated conditions like the amount of screen time and total time on set. From a contractual perspective, I didn't care. However, I would have to become not just a Prussian social theorist but a German Gypsy. It would be challenging and exciting but I was keen to understand how the roles would be allocated. Presumably Daniel would take the lead Gypsy male parts. The discussion had not taken account of me being a member of the cast.

They were talking to me as a friend and confidant. I stated the obvious by saying Elliot would have to be consulted. James agreed and disappeared into the bedroom to make the call.

"Nick," James said upon re-entering the lounge room after a good half an hour on the phone to the producer, "Elliot thinks this is by far the best way to go with the production, but he's also concerned. You've nailed this one characterization, but do you think you could do others as well? It wouldn't make sense to progress with this idea if we can't have all the cast involved."

I said I'd read the Gaurige scenes again that evening and do a further audition tomorrow, if that's what James would like. If I wasn't ready, he should just let me know. James smiled and thanked me for my understanding.

"Let's drink to our level-headed Herr Engels!"

I stayed up half the night working through the script. The Gypsy dialogue was different in rhythm and meter. It was more colloquial and fast-paced than the more formal sentence structures James had given Asarov, Marx, Engels, and Jenny. James had drawn the Gauriges as clever but uneducated. They spoke in clipped tones and short sentences. They were always laughing or fighting. The family relationships were based on a patriarchal model that involved endless internal squabbling. Asarov was surely re-telling her own history, although the script was silent on this point. Despite the arguments and male posturing, the Gaurige men generally did as they were asked, either by the father, the mother, their sisters, or wives.

There were two roles that were of particular interest to me.

The Gaurige patriarch, Henry, was a roguish arch-villain. It was he who stumbled upon the legislative loophole that allowed him to acquire his first landholding. While it was the principal Gaurige role, and perhaps best suited to someone of Daniel's experience, I wanted to read for it. The other was that of Henry's oldest daughter's husband. He desperately wanted to be allowed into the scam but was kept at a distance by his father-in-law who suspected the younger man wanted to take over as head of the family.

Either role would suit me, I thought, although I appreciated they both required an entirely different characterization to that of Engels. In capturing Engels, you could say I placed an equal emphasis on nineteenth-century formality, a sharp and inquiring mindfulness, and a dry but quick-witted sense of humour. All these attributes were alluded to in the screenplay, but it was up to me to bring them together.

However, I could see the Gypsy roles would require a focus on theatricality and physicality. The scenes were either outside in the forest or inside extravagant Gypsy caravans. Unlike the staid Victorian era, there was a quickness and sense of the human that would need to come across, not to mention the ability to fight and wrestle. It occurred to me that transforming myself into a Gypsy, should James and Elliot think I was up to it, would be far easier if the shoots were done separately. That is, if the London scenes were completed in their entirety before we moved on to the Gauriges.

By the early hours of the morning I had memorized what I needed to. I fell asleep wondering what Daniel, Kate, and Tilda would make of it all.

Elliot picked us up the next morning. The producer was nervous about what the cast might say about taking on additional roles, but he was laughing and mischievously looking forward to reactions that might, if he wasn't careful, derail the project.

"If they all violently disagree," he said, "we can stick with the original plan and sign up some Germans."

I sensed Elliot doubted my ability to take my acting further than I had achieved with Engels, notwithstanding how positive he had been about my first audition. I wasn't overly concerned. I had nothing to lose. When thinking about how I might approach, say, the role of the Gaurige son-in-law, I again recalled *The Last of the Mohicans* in which Day Lewis played a white man raised as an American Indian. I thought I could use Daniel's example as a guide to getting *inside* the Gypsy type, which was variously anxious, impatient, confident, and jealous. I would tackle it in a more physical way and be bolder with my facial expressions.

We arrived at the studio and entered the rehearsal room. Kate was the only actor there. She talked briefly about the charity event she'd attended the previous evening where she'd sat at a table with Tony Blair, the former British Prime Minister, and his wife, Cherie. Her table had raised over two hundred thousand pounds, with Giorgio Armani matching the contribution. Twenty thousand was raised through the sale of a dress Kate wore in *Titanic*.

"These things can be a drag," Kate said, "but they are for good causes. Tilda didn't make it to the fundraiser after all—she's mercurial don't you think?"

I didn't have time to offer an opinion. As she was finishing the story, Daniel and Tilda arrived, at which point James asked everyone to sit down. I could tell they were wondering why Elliot had appeared for what was just another read through.

James announced, without inviting questions or input from the group, they would be taking on the roles of the Gaurige Gypsies, in addition to those we'd been rehearsing. He gave a more detailed account of the rationale he'd provided to Claire and me the previous evening. He emphasized the importance of the wonderful Asarov imagination but how he didn't want to depict it in that way. From a theatrical, ensemble perspective it would work wonderfully, and the new approach would provide a richness that would otherwise, he thought, be unachievable.

As one, the three actors stood up and applauded. They were clearly looking forward to the challenge and complexity of playing multiple characters.

★

Kate thought it made perfect sense to use the cast in the way James suggested. She offered her take on Viktoria Asarov.

"You see," she said, "Viktoria has a cloistered existence in St Petersburg. At any moment her Gypsy lineage could be discovered—and with terrible consequences. James, you don't step that out in your screenplay, but I don't think you need to. She lives alone, she works in a library, she is a writer, and she admires Karl Marx. These are hardly the attributes of a normal young woman who might more sensibly be on the lookout for a husband and financial security, especially so in an era when women were so vulnerable without a man to support them. Having said that, her vulnerability is complemented by an inner strength and intellectual confidence. Like many nineteenth-century women she is inexperienced in the ways of the world because of her inability to participate fully in it—but Viktoria makes up for that by imagining her own worlds and impossible adventures. So it makes sense she would use the people around her to build the Gypsy personas. I can't believe, James, you only just thought of this. It's brilliant!"

Daniel Day Lewis, speaking in his heavy German accent, suggested Asarov would have imagined Marx as Henry Gaurige and Jenny as Henry's wife.

"It occurs to me," he said, "that Engels, as one of the calmer influences in Asarov's life, would be imagined by her as one of the sons, or more than one of the sons. Viktoria would surely have imagined herself as the oldest daughter. Marx could also play the daughter's husband, the one who seeks to head up the family against the wishes of Henry."

Tilda didn't agree with Day Lewis at all.

"Well, my dearest Karl," she said, turning to the great actor, "that would mean you taking on the three principal Gypsy roles. Don't you think that's overdoing it a bit? As we all know, and as young James has made clear all along, the film is about Asarov's imagination and her secret writing. No, it is Asarov who should be center stage and so perhaps the best thing to do is ask her! Dear Viktoria...who do you think should be cast as which Gaurige?"

There was a brief pause before Kate, or Viktoria, responded.

"Well, I don't think it's as simple as all that. There's no need to have a definitive answer. Asarov would surely have seen different faces in different Gauriges at different times. If we want to make this film as truly great as I think it can be, we should prepare to take on all roles depending on the state of the characters' relationships in the Marx household. What do you think?"

James, who with Elliot had remained silent during this part of the conversation, said Kate's reasoning was entirely correct.

"Anyway," he concluded, "there are only a few of you to share around so you will *have* to take on more than one role. And, as Kate seems to be suggesting, I think both Karl *and* Friedrich could share the role of Henry. We will all have to adapt."

★

Sensibly, we put discussions about who would play which role to one side, with James explaining we would do the filming in three parts. The first would be the Marx-Asarov scenes in London. The second would be the Gauriges, and the third would cover Viktoria in St Petersburg. The plan was meant to ensure we could concentrate on getting the atmosphere right for each situation.

"You are all very talented," he exclaimed, "but I don't want any confusion!"

Daniel Day Lewis said, in his pitch-perfect German, "Ich stimme mit dir überein, das ist eine sehr gute Idee."

From that point on, rehearsals couldn't have gone better. Having a small cast meant James could work with us individually, but his suggestions were confined largely to timing, movement, and intensity. As we finished up with a final read-through, Tilda came over to me as we left the studio. She put her arm through mine and pulled me to her as if she needed to keep warm. Tilda asked if I wanted to go for a drink at a pub, the White Horse, not far from Pinewood, so she could talk to me about working in front of the camera

"My dear Nick," she said, "you have done very well. You have exceeded my expectations. But acting on set where there will be dozens of people—camera assistants, assistant directors, production staff, gaffers, lighting technicians—may be a challenge. Perhaps, I could give you a few tips over a drink and light supper."

I was grateful for the offer. Tilda went to her car and told the driver he wouldn't be needed again that evening. We got into mine, and Tilda issued directions. It only took a few minutes. We were driving quickly, even dangerously, on the narrow country roads.

The pub, though nearly empty apart from Tilda and me, felt claustrophobic. It was hundreds of years old and designed for people no taller than children. We ordered red wine and spaghetti. As soon as the plates arrived Tilda pushed hers to one side, concentrating instead on her glass of wine. She talked about the challenges of working on set, and joked that at least there were no nude scenes.

"Most directors at some point like getting you naked in a room full of people," she commented, "but thankfully this is a film without any sex! It's implicit, of course, that there is something going on between Asarov and Marx, but nothing *explicit*. It's a great tension, don't you think?"

Tilda remarked she had nothing against on-screen nudity *per se*, but that European directors had a far more sophisticated approach than their American counterparts, which she said tended to be gratuitous rather than having any essential connection to the story. She leaned back in her seat and put her feet on my lap. Tilda had taken off her shoes. I was taken aback, not knowing whether she was seducing me or making fun of me. Actors have a quality about them you don't encounter in a normal workplace.

By way of example, I had noticed a lot of physicality, touching, and even familial kissing, between the actors. Daniel was an exception but even he behaved somewhat affectionately in his own Prussianesque style. There seemed to be a custom, at least on the set of *The Secret Writer* and perhaps it was the same in other film productions, of behaving like you were all part of a close family. While my first meeting with the team had been, from my perspective, slightly awkward, all subsequent interactions involved an assumed closeness or intimacy I found difficult to get used to. I had nothing against it. It was just that in the office people kept a polite distance from each other even though most of us had known and worked with each other for years.

It occurred to me at that moment, with Tilda Swinton gazing into my eyes and rubbing her feet on my thighs, how important intimacy was on a film set. At the office you have plenty of time to get to know people, while the making of a film is concentrated and time limited. You need to feel comfortable and relaxed with your colleagues from the very start. In the business development team, if you were to assume the closeness of a family, it would be difficult to maintain over long periods. It was safer to be professional and friendly, but relatively distant. But in the acting world I'd noticed during rehearsal how everyone congratulated each other at every opportunity. I didn't mind it. In fact, I quite enjoyed it. Back in Sydney there were moments of appreciation from your supervisors, but they were infrequent and forced.

All of a sudden, and with a perhaps overly dramatic flourish, Tilda raised her glass.

"To *The Secret Writer* and the newest member of the acting community!" She leaned over the table and asked if I felt like a nightcap.

In the back of the car, Tilda pulled a packet of filterless cigarettes from her tiny handbag. She smoked while she rested her head on my shoulder. Her hair was transparent-red, her skin a ghostly white.

"Nick," she said, "I hope you know what you're in for...the hard work only begins with the making of a movie. Everything gets more difficult when it's finished. You have to travel around, promote it, go to awards nights, and all the rest of it. Read your contract carefully because there will be a year of commitments to attend to."

Tilda threw her cigarette to the ground as the driver opened the car door in front of a quaint English country cottage. It had a thatched roof and looked rather charming. She put her arm in mine and led me inside. There was an open suitcase in the hallway. Tilda poured a whiskey and took me to her bedroom without waiting for me to drink it. At three in the morning she told me to leave. We were, after all, required on set for makeup and costume in just over an hour. My car was still waiting outside.

During the short drive to Pinewood, it occurred to me I might fall in love with Tilda. While I hardly knew her I felt we had connected deeply. However, despite what happened she'd given no hint she felt anything. While reliving the evening I'd spent with her, with both excitement and trepidation about what might follow, I noticed another email from the Executive Director. He apologized for sending two emails in only a few days but thought it necessary to update me on some ideas the Chief Operating Officer had put on the table. The Executive Director wanted my views on their practicality and how quickly they could be implemented.

It turned out the new ideas were consistent with the original recommendations, but went even further. I should have been preparing myself mentally for the shoot, but what was being proposed was interesting. The COO wanted a staff rotation system. People would be moved between teams for three to six month periods. This would enable individuals to build their skills, engage more broadly with their colleagues throughout the company, and have a much better understanding of the business overall. It was hard to disagree with the logic. Our report had suggested the company adopt a strategic approach to building a culture of continuous improvement. Simply bringing Claire on board had brought a new perspective and fresh ideas. So, based on that reasoning, giving staff different experiences and opportunities would, I thought, have a similar but longer-term impact.

The second proposal referred specifically to me. There would be a new Strategy Team which would take on the combined functions of business development and contracts. The Executive Director had mentioned this in his earlier email. However, the new team would have two additional functions —corporate planning and reporting—and have responsibility not just for sales and contractual arrangements but for setting the strategic direction of the firm and internal communications. Those who might have been considered excess under the restructure could be allocated roles in the new team, should they have the capability and willingness to do so. Given the number of deliverables, Strategy would have its own director who would become part of the Executive team. The final part of his email read, "Nick, we would like you to head up the new team, and if you can convince Claire to return then all the better. Take your time in making your decision—and don't say no too quickly! You can nominate your salary as long as it's not more than mine!"

I was flattered by the offer but had no time to consider it. The car pulled up at the studio and I was led to a large makeup room. It was hot inside, the enormous mirrors framed by bright fluorescent lights.

I was taken to a barber's chair in front of which was a photograph of Friedrich Engels stuck to the mirror. The makeup artists called me Mr Clement. One by one Kate, Daniel, and Tilda entered the room. I turned to Tilda but she only said a general good morning to everyone. There was little conversation as we were transformed into our nineteenth-century characters.

By the time I was asked to stand up and go to wardrobe, I could hardly recognize myself. My hair was thick and grey and I had a full but well-trimmed beard. I had aged ten years, with wrinkles around my eyes and mouth and age spots painted onto my hands. I looked very much like the Engels in the photograph that guided the work of the makeup artists. I noticed Kate and Tilda had been given wigs, their hair tied back in the Victorian style, but other than that they didn't look appreciably different. Unlike me, they didn't need the same amount of cosmetic overlay.

Although Daniel spent about the same amount of time in the makeup chair and gave frequent directions to the makeup artists in his thick German accent, he looked very much like he did in the first days of rehearsal when he'd already looked so much like Karl Marx.

The wardrobe area was the size of a warehouse, with thousands of garments hanging on endless rows of hangers. I was again addressed as Mr Clement by the head of the department. He pulled a suit from the rack, above which was a large sign— *The Secret Writer*. There were at least a dozen full-length dresses in muted cream, greys, browns, and light blues. Each was assigned to either Ms Winslet or Ms Swinton. My three-piece wool suit didn't look so different from the one Daniel Day Lewis had chosen. I stood on a box while adjustments were quickly made to my trousers and jacket sleeves.

Kate and Tilda were having petticoats and dresses lowered over their heads by a team of assistants. They, too, looked as if they were from another century. Tilda was speaking to herself, going over her lines.

We were just about ready when James walked in to check on preparations. He drew us together into a circle with our arms around each other's shoulders. Tilda was opposite me and looked directly into my eyes for the duration of James' introductory remarks, as if daring me to look away. Our director spoke to each of us in turn, looking into our eyes to ensure his words of advice would have a lasting impact on our performances.

"Viktoria," he said, "you are supremely talented, yet vulnerable and lost, but there is a great hope inside you and you never give up. Karl, you are a genius but with such a limited emotional range it's impossible for you to accept greatness in others. Jenny, you love your husband, who for all his faults is generous and a good husband and father. However, the closeness between him and Viktoria is killing you. Friedrich, James concluded, turning to me in the huddle, you are the voice of reason. You are invisible but essential. Your only fault is you failed to understand how badly Viktoria was being treated. Perhaps you ignored it until it was too late."

James led the way to the set. Tilda secretly pinched my arm in what I took to be a sign of affection and reassurance.

I thought I'd prepared myself mentally for such an environment but I was taken aback by the scale of the production. There were hundreds of people busily making sure the final details were all in place, with cameras manned by chief and assistant cameramen and other technical assistants. There were electricians, lighting technicians, and grips, whose role it was to move the cameras by pulling them on rails. Continuity staff circled to take photographs every few minutes so that our hair, clothes, and makeup were consistent from shot to shot. The same people who'd helped us get ready were on set all day, touching up our appearance at every opportunity.

The interior of Marx's house was entirely convincing. The furniture, carpets, and household decorations made me feel like I had been transported to another time. I felt the acute responsibility of ensuring my performance matched the quality of the production. I closed my eyes and found myself disappearing into Friedrich Engels. I spoke my lines silently to myself and started to feel a great warmth for my great friend, Marx. I also felt deeply for Jenny, who I knew would be suffering terribly from her husband's insensitivity. How could he behave in such a way?

In spite of my preparations, I wasn't needed on set until late in the day when Marx was asking my opinion about employing Asarov. I decided to use the time to send an email to the Executive Director back in Sydney.

I stepped out of Friedrich Engels, or perhaps he stepped out of me. It's difficult to describe the transition. It was a strangely involuntary process. Perhaps you could describe it as simultaneously shedding a skin while slipping into another. As I returned to myself, I considered whether Tilda's cold behavior was a feature of her characterization rather than reflective of her attitude towards me. She could have been channelling Jenny's state of mind and this may perhaps have invaded her personal territory. However, as soon as the thought occurred to me I discounted it. Tilda Swinton didn't seem to approach her work in the same way as Daniel. She always retained her *self,* while simultaneously being able to inhabit her character. She had a tremendous subtlety I found both mysterious and charming. Tilda brought this quality to her Jenny, who she played with a tenderness and inner strength that were perfect for her relationship with her on-screen husband.

Kate Winslet on the other hand didn't have that same fragility. She displayed a certain toughness both in and out of character. Daniel Day Lewis was different again. Contrary to what I experienced when I first met him, when I found him generous and fascinating, he'd become inscrutable. As soon as he'd become Karl Marx, it was impossible to get through to him. Although I could have relaxed in my dressing room until called, I preferred to stay on set and watch my colleagues in action and how James managed operations. He engaged most closely with the actors and the director of photography while various assistants did the running around providing secondary instructions to others who would run off and tell someone else. Everyone used hand-held radio communication devices, or ear pieces connected wirelessly to small units attached to their clothing.

I saw Claire sitting at a table some distance from the cameras. She was working on a laptop finalizing costings for Elliot. I sat down beside her and worked up my response to the Executive Director. While Claire was dismissive of me engaging with him at all, it would have been discourteous if I hadn't responded to his generous job offer. It was tempting, to say the least, and worthy of serious consideration.

★

Reflecting on the Executive Director's email, I thought it was a positive move to have a system where staff could move between teams. I agreed that one of the firm's problems was a tendency for staff to concentrate only on their own work units, becoming too focused on their own projects without getting a proper understanding of the rest of the business at a holistic level. In particular, it was hard for staff to fully understand how their work contributed to broader strategic outcomes.

In my response, I described how, despite the imperative of getting people to work together and contribute holistically, if you were going to implement some sort of rotation system, you might want to start by targeting certain staff with specific capabilities who were seen as having potential. If you approached staff rotation in that way, I wrote, you could demonstrate how it would develop career pathways. If you didn't adopt a planned approach, you might be placing people in teams in which they had no interest, or you might be moving them to functional areas where you might not be making the best use of their skills. There was a further consideration I emphasized to the Executive Director.

I explained that while there were obvious benefits to staff mobility, it needed to be balanced with team *stability*. It would be necessary to carefully plan when people would be transferred. For example, it might not be practical at certain times within the business cycle. Annual reporting was always a period of considerable pressure (although, through my recent experience with Claire, I could see how the process could be made much simpler) and there would be no point in moving experienced people who were involved in mission-critical functions without a gradual on-boarding of less experienced staff. In my view, the proposal would be counter-productive if it wasn't mapped out properly and staff didn't have a say in system design.

Another idea suddenly came to me. I suggested a formal staff consultation mechanism. You might, I suggested, introduce an internal social media platform, where staff could put up ideas for how to improve the business or reduce costs. This could be aligned with a reward and recognition program that could be part of performance development—something which most staff and managers gave scant consideration to. If there were a financial or other reward such as attendance at an interstate conference or something of that nature, people would be far more likely to contribute and engage.

I signed off by saying I was in no position to either accept or decline the offer of the new Director role, and reminded him I would be away for at least a few more months. Of course, although front of mind, I didn't say that I had no idea whether I wanted to become a full-time actor. As soon as I sent the email I realized my suggestions may make him even more keen to bring me back.

★

James commanded the room like a general. Every one of his requests was dealt with quickly, professionally, and with a minimum of fuss. Of course, it was my first experience watching actors work in front of cameras, but the quality of the performances can't be overstated. Not surprisingly, I felt a degree of pressure when I was called up by James at the end of the day. Everyone would have known I had no background in the dramatic arts, not to mention training. Any slip or missed line would have been embarrassing. Although I was sure the crew were just going about their jobs, it felt like all eyes were on me, hoping I would fail.

I stepped past two men gaffer-taping electrical cords to the floor, walked past the director, and into Marx's sitting room. The makeup artists retouched my face and hair and someone from continuity took photographs. Marx was already in the room sitting in an armchair. James would film me opening and stepping through the door at a later stage. For the moment, we would work on the basis I had arrived, been greeted by the housemaid, and shown upstairs to where Marx was waiting.

When the cameras weren't rolling, there was nonetheless considerable activity in the studio. However as soon as James put his right hand in the air, everyone became silent and focused. After the director checked everyone was ready and there was silence on set, one of the assistants held the clapperboard, shouted *Scene Two Charlie, Take One*, and snapped it shut. James waited a moment before calling *action*. My first appearance was only for a few minutes. I saw Claire looking at me from behind one of the cameras, smiling with encouragement. She looked as nervous as I felt. Daniel Day Lewis and I did three takes, I think for my benefit more than his. There is no doubt that, although I had no problem with my lines I was, quite literally, still finding my feet in terms of presence on set and knowing exactly where to be.

Silence after each take indicated the director was happy and we could move on to the next. In fact, however, ours was the final shot of the day and James called Day Lewis and me over to look at the *rushes*, an industry term for the raw footage of what's just been filmed. James didn't say anything to indicate he wasn't happy with the performances and Tilda and Kate, standing behind us, murmured their approval. We hugged each other and Tilda and Kate kissed me and Daniel on the cheek.

James thanked everyone for their hard work. He reminded the cast and crew of tomorrow's 4am call. Before we broke up there was a round of applause. It was a significant moment. The first day had gone relatively smoothly, much to the relief of the director and his team.

It was early evening. I looked across to Tilda but she seemed to be thinking about things other than me.

✳

I waited for Tilda outside the studio but when she emerged looking beautiful in an all-white outfit, she didn't acknowledge me. She climbed into her car and disappeared. Given Tilda's disappearance to wherever she was going, I was happy to see Claire, who asked if she could share a ride with a famous actor. We drove back to the apartment in silence and I could tell she had something on her mind. When we were comfortably in our apartment sipping white wine, Claire, smoking a cigarette in the lounge room because she said that now we were in the movie industry we could do whatever we wanted, complimented me on my performance.

"Nick," she said, "I don't want to go on about it but you are easily matching Daniel, Tilda, and Kate. I must say, Kate's Viktoria is a wonderful thing to behold. She brings out her intelligence and strength in a way that does perfect justice to the script. Do you remember how you talked about the story being about the *writing*? Well, Tilda and Kate have this ability not only to give themselves completely to their characters, but have you also noticed how they never allow their performances to drive the story? Instead, they operate just behind the text and allow the narrative to reveal itself rather than them being the focus. It's extraordinary, Nick. Whether you are trying to or not, you are doing the same thing and your acting has the same subtle impact on the *showing* of the story. You are the agent of the text rather than the voice of it. It's hard to explain but the actor should be behind the action, not quite part of it. Does that make any sense at all?"

What she'd described made perfect sense to me, and I agreed with her views about Tilda and Kate's performances. I suggested they seemed expert in holding themselves back. I reminded Claire that at different times both actors had halted the filming because their performances were becoming too *theatrical,* which was the word Tilda used on more than one occasion to chastise herself. Then, collecting themselves mentally and physically, you could see how they made their characterizations more flat and even. There is certainly a fine balance between *becoming* the character and at the same time maintaining a level of self-awareness so you can react and alter the performance should you need to. In many ways it is a craft that defies explanation.

Claire thought it remarkable how the actor's fame can be made to disappear or dissolve, or at least become smaller as they grow into their roles. She thought it counter-intuitive but true nevertheless. Claire wasn't quite so sure Daniel Day Lewis had quite the same ability.

"I could be wrong," she said, "but I think you need to talk to him, or perhaps it would be better if James did."

I felt quite uncomfortable at that point in the conversation. Not only did I disagree with Claire, there was simply no way an actor of my limited experience could talk to Daniel about his profession. I couldn't fault his acting. I suggested to Claire that if anyone were to talk to Daniel (and I didn't see the need for it in any case) it should be James. It would be impossible for anyone to give a finer performance.

Claire hadn't seen much of James lately. He'd been spending extra time with Kate who was having difficulty with her Russian accent, while Claire had been busy working for Elliot. I found it hard to believe Kate was struggling. Our voice coach had worked with us already and I hadn't noticed any problems, either during rehearsal or on the first day of filming. Certainly, no-one had said anything.

After pouring another glass of wine, Claire changed the subject. She asked about the emails I had been getting from the Executive Director. I explained how our report, the recommendations of which were being implemented in full, was being used as a rationale for an even more significant structural shift. The new Chief Operating Officer wasn't going to be satisfied with limiting changes to those we had recommended. She wanted to roll out initiatives that would go much further in promoting staff engagement, cross-team collaboration, and career development.

"The firm should be careful not to do too much too quickly," Claire suggested, "because it could be a recipe for disaster. You can't just flick a switch and expect everything to improve overnight."

She reminded me of one section of our report that went into some detail about staged implementation strategies. I told Claire about the job offer, but she didn't say anything because her phone rang. It was Elliot. Claire took the phone to her bedroom and when she returned had lost interest in what we'd been discussing.

Late that evening I received a parcel of books that Daniel had had couriered to our apartment. Inside the heavy cardboard box were books on method acting by Brooks, Hagen, Stanislawski, and Blumenfeld. I couldn't believe how thoughtful this was given he was so deep in character. It seemed, for my benefit, he had made an exception to his normal creative practice. I went to bed with the intention of reading one of the discourses on acting but instead fell asleep and dreamed about Daniel Day Lewis.

In the dream, Daniel and I were on an outdoor adventure. We were in rural Uruguay outside Montevideo. We emerged from a dense rainforest, tired but happy in each other's company. We came across a small town where we decided to stay for the night. Daniel and I took a room at the hotel. It was old and dirty. The sheets were heavy like sails.

We started up a conversation with the owner and his wife. There were children running everywhere and we had to raise our voices to be heard. Daniel commented on their fine family. The couple proceeded to tell us a long story about how it was indeed a fine and very large family, but it wasn't complete because their oldest son, who would have been ten years old if he was still with them, had disappeared several years ago.

Daniel asked about the circumstances of the boy's disappearance. The boy had failed to return from school where he had been a good student and very popular. The police were hopeless. They had given up the investigation after a few days of asking stupid questions.

The wife of the hotelier made us a delicious meal of open grilled-beef sandwiches on flatbread. Her husband poured us two giant glasses of red wine. Daniel offered to look for the boy. The couple protested it would be hopeless but eventually agreed no harm could be done by undertaking one further search. I asked what the boy's name was. The woman said her son's name was Luis Aragonés.

We finished our meal and went to bed.

We woke in pools of sweat. The humidity was stultifying but Daniel insisted we fulfil our promise and continue the search the local police had so lazily abandoned. Upon reaching the forest we'd walked through the previous day, we found a young boy sitting under a tree. It was not two minutes from the hotel. He was eating an exotic fruit, the aroma of which reminded me of burning petrol. Daniel asked him his name. The boy said his name was Luis Aragonés.

We took Luis back to the hotel. His parents were naturally pleased to see their boy. They gave him a meal and before long he was running around with the rest of the children, who seemed to have grown in number. There are other details that come to mind such as walking over a long and perilous bridge made only of rope and having long conversations with policemen that all came to nothing. The narrative didn't make sense. It occurred to me that the dream was about wanting to get closer to the great actor, and that the Uruguayan family were the Gypsies in *The Secret Writer*.

I woke to find the apartment empty. I went downstairs to find my driver waiting for me. I felt an urgent need to see Tilda.

After a busy but successful morning I asked Tilda to have lunch with me. She said it would have to be quick because she needed to prepare for a difficult scene. We were going to shoot a dramatic, ten-minute sequence where Jenny von Westphalen questions her husband's behavior towards Asarov. In rehearsal, Tilda had given Jenny a certain authority in her relationship with Marx, but it was one that could unravel at any moment. You might describe the characterization as bold, but brittle, stoicism. Jenny was too proud to walk away from her marriage (an unlikely scenario in Victorian times) but she was also too proud not to demand an explanation for the long hours Marx spent alone with Asarov.

Jenny's authority, demonstrated by a humble intelligence and a mastery of household matters, was undermined by a Victorian subservience to her husband. Marx's explanations were lofty and high-minded. He was incapable of understanding the pressure that his relationship with the young Russian was placing on his marriage.

While Jenny saw nothing physical between them (and the screenplay didn't specifically indicate the presence or absence of a sexual relationship), what she witnessed was even worse—an intellectual intimacy that was theirs' alone. In short, she wanted Asarov gone. Marx refused, citing the need to complete his major work. In rehearsal, I'd noticed the emotional impact of this scene on Tilda. She appeared to be struggling to hold Jenny's obvious discomfort in check.

No sooner had we sat down in the cafeteria than Tilda suddenly changed her mind and suggested we postpone and have dinner that evening. She knew what I was going to ask her.

"Don't worry," she laughed, "everyone talks about Daniel—he's very famous, you know."

It was Tilda, Daniel, and I who featured most in the rest of the day's work. The scene Tilda was so keen to prepare for was completed in one take. When it was over the entire cast and crew gave her a standing ovation. Daniel applauded and said *das war eine ausgezeichnete Leistung meine liebe Dame.* Tilda looked even paler than her usual pallid self as she walked from the set. She seemed diminished by the force of the performance.

I had a number of shorter appearances including one where I discussed with Jenny the merits of Marx having an assistant. I noticed something between Engels and Marx's wife that I hadn't before. There was a frisson that suggested if she and Marx couldn't reconcile their differences, there may be a place for Engels in her life.

I went to my dressing room to collect my annotated copy of the screenplay. On top of it was a red envelope with my name on it. Inside was a note from Tilda in which she had written, somewhat mysteriously, that she hoped I was beginning to understand the job a little better and we should catch up that evening. Of course, I wanted to talk about Daniel, but I was also understandably keen to understand the strength of her feelings for me.

Tilda was waiting in the doorway of her home as my car drove off. She was dressed in a Bon Jovi t-shirt and jeans. She led me to the kitchen. Tilda had prepared a beetroot, rocket, walnut, tomato, and goat's curd salad. There was a Sicilian balsamic and honey dressing which she assured me I would like very much. She poured the wine and laid two strips of beef in a pan, frying them on each side for about fifteen seconds before placing them on white plates and carrying them to the dining table. We ate quickly without saying anything.

Tilda lit a cigarette and went to make coffee. Sitting in the lounge room of the small house in two very comfortable armchairs, she asked why I wanted to talk about Daniel Day Lewis. I answered it was probably nothing but I'd noticed something between James and Daniel, and even between her and Daniel. Tilda crossed her legs. She suggested that I didn't want to talk about Daniel Day Lewis—what I really wanted to talk about was acting because that was the issue at hand, not Daniel.

"He's not the only actor in the world," she said. "You see, acting means different things to different people and is sometimes given too much importance. Your method will inform the characterization but overall the intention remains the same. That is, to become someone else in order to reveal something to the audience. The nature of the relationship between actor and audience is not well understood, and a lot of academic work is being done to better understand audience experience."

Tilda became a little esoteric when she said one of the most interesting lines of academic inquiry is the investigation of the space between the performance and those experiencing it, its invisibility, and endless possibilities and potential. I had no understanding of such a concept and said nothing. Tilda was in full flight and I found her views fascinating. They reflected James' to some extent but obviously came from a person with far more experience in the industry.

"The dramatic art of acting," she concluded, "is only a small part of what we call the spectacle of entertainment and acting success can be described in different ways. For example, I hope when I perform, the person you know as me temporarily diminishes to the point where I can most effectively be a voice for the intentions of the author or director. For me that is success. For others, the critical success factor might be, as it is for Daniel Day Lewis and many others in our profession, the total *becoming* of the character. The issue of course, not that it ultimately matters much because most people who watch popular movies are not well-versed in the arts, is that rather than a *characterization,* what is produced is just a larger version of the actor. What I want to emphasize, my darling Nick, is it's the auteur's vision that the audience should be able to experience, not the quality of the acting. Daniel will never understand this. He probably did once but I doubt he ever will again. Having said that, I don't think it will be a problem. *The Secret Writer* will be a success, I can promise you that."

Tilda let me stay with her until the morning. I was of course relieved my feelings for her were reciprocated. She dropped me at my Pinewood accommodation. Claire was already up and clearly hadn't slept well. I could tell she knew about my new relationship. Claire told me to get ready so we could go to the studio. It was obvious James had already left or slept elsewhere.

I had my suspicions but was reluctant to speculate.

Claire reminded me that after today there would be a three day break because Kate had other commitments that predated her signing on for *The Secret Writer*. Claire would also be away, with Elliot, for at least a week. She almost demanded, you might describe it as a tirade, that I speak to James about Daniel Day Lewis. I pointed out, echoing Tilda's take on the profession she'd outlined the night before, there are many different approaches to acting and it wouldn't be right for people as inexperienced as us to try and influence the direction of the film or individual performances.

Unusually for me, I lost my patience by asking Claire what she even knew about acting. Claire answered, in a tone that betrayed her frustration and even anger, that while she may not be an industry professional it was obvious to her that James' fears at the beginning of the whole adventure were going to be realized. In fact, she warned they may have *already* been realized. Claire became even more dramatic. She'd been hearing about James' film-making ideas from the first day she met him—about the primacy of the text—and she pointed out that it was I who had first understood the true meaning of *The Secret Writer*.

"It's a brilliant piece," she said, "but it was you who appreciated the importance of the writing and why you would need sensitive actors to realize its full potential."

I could see my friend was holding back tears. Still, she went on. "James is unhappy with aspects of the performance and rightly so," she complained. "But he says nothing because he finds himself in a world where he can have a relationship with someone like Kate Winslet. I don't blame him. Kate is beautiful and intelligent, and a wonderful actor."

I didn't have time to respond because, on receipt of a text message, Claire raced downstairs to Elliot's car. I saw them lean into each other like long-separated lovers. It seemed on the one hand Claire was criticizing the production but on the other having a relationship with the man who was, to a significant degree, responsible for what she now thought was a second rate Hollywood movie.

Although production of *The Secret Writer* had given rise to significant complexities driven by new relationships and disparate observations about the acting craft, it moved swiftly ahead. James maintained his composure and spent an increasing amount of time with Daniel Day Lewis. Daniel's performance was almost imperceptibly developing into a different type of characterization. While in that first week I could never fault his Karl Marx, Daniel's acting was now becoming more nuanced. He was more relaxed and even started to have fun on set by deliberately saying the wrong lines or hamming it up by taking Jenny in his arms. He had a very good sense of humor and these moments broke up the tension to the benefit of both cast and crew.

Presumably, Daniel understood he was altering a method that had served him so well. Whether he did was of no real consequence. He was now more at ease with the rest of the cast, and the crew picked up on it too. Now, when Daniel needed to ask a point of clarification with James, he would speak in his normal Irish-British-American accent. He didn't seem to feel the need to inhabit Marx in the same way. I wanted Claire to see the new Daniel in action. If it were true (and I suspected it was) that James had been dissatisfied with where the film was heading, or where Marx was being taken, then he had masterfully and subtly directed Daniel into a new way of working.

It was becoming clear to me how little I knew about acting. There were moments when I was confident I was fitting in with those around me, but seeing the way Daniel was able to adapt his characterization and professional habits of many years to ensure the requisite tension and focus on the text was incredibly impressive. It was also obvious Claire had greatly underestimated James' skill as a director and perhaps this was one factor in why their relationship, which had appeared unbreakable, was coming to an end.

I reflected on the rumors that get reported in the newspapers every day about famous people and how there were so many obstacles to a long-lasting relationship. For example, the film industry could keep people apart for months at a time. It would be almost impossible to manage schedules that allowed for meaningful time together. There was also the issue of onset intimacy that only those involved in a project could understand. From that first day, we'd all worked so closely together on a creative endeavour where you need to share ideas and bounce off each other for artistic inspiration. The relationship between us all, and with key technical staff, had to be strong and constructive. I realized it was inevitable this could lead to romantic attachments such as those that had developed between Tilda and me, and Kate and James. Even Elliot and Claire were now together.

Despite all these developments we were ahead of schedule, which I found out was almost unheard of in the film industry. James put this down to the excellence of his entire team, and that the shoot had so far been relatively straightforward and entirely undertaken in the studio where lighting and other factors are easier to manage.

At the end of that last day of filming, everyone wished Kate well because she was flying to the south of France to film a *Longines* commercial. She apologized for interrupting everything but James assured her there was nothing to be concerned about. After a frantic period which included fast-tracking a screenplay into a fully-fledged production complete with cast and crew, he was also looking forward to a break. James might also fly to Europe to get some sun.

Kate and James left together for a teleconference with Elliot.

Tilda straightened my hair with the palm of her transparent hand and asked me what we should do with our time off, then suggesting we take one of the cars and drive to Scotland where she lived just outside Edinburgh. I readily agreed. She asked whether I'd ever been to Ireland because, apparently, I must be Irish. I said I'd never been outside Australia. Tilda had noticed how I always put my Claddagh ring back on straight after filming and assumed I had some connection with that country.

On the way to Scotland, I received an email from the Executive Director. The Chief Operating Officer had been copied in. The earlier communications I'd received were updates on the change process and reminders I was welcome to return at the end of my sabbatical to take up an executive opportunity. This time, attached to the email was a draft change management plan that ran to thirty pages. I opened the document and saw, based on the index, a detailed transition plan for moving from the current business model to a new, collaborative way of working. There was a chart that stepped out timeframes for each stage in the process, starting with a communications strategy for informing staff about the changes.

The plan set out a staff workshop timetable and how, more informally and anonymously, staff could send thoughts and ideas to a dedicated email address. While I had only glanced at the document on my iPhone, I could see it was a far more detailed and expert articulation of the recommendations Claire and I had drafted. The firm had engaged a change management consultant to write up the plan based on a two-day executive workshop. I thought it an unusual approach because that was one of the disciplines we specialized in. Having said that, I could see the value in having an independent perspective. Someone once told me you have to *bring in the outside to change things from the inside.*

Meanwhile, Tilda was driving at a terrific speed while hardly looking at the road. She asked what I was reading. I gave Tilda a quick overview of where the plan was going. She asked me a number of questions about the change management process wanting to know what the timeframes were, how many people would be impacted, whether they would all be involved in the consultations, and most importantly, the principal objective of the restructure. These were remarkably well-informed questions given they had come from an actress with, presumably, little experience of the consultancy world.

I explained I'd only just received the transition plan and hadn't read the whole document but I knew it was looking at an eighteen month transition timeframe. Ninety staff would be impacted. The principal objectives were structural efficiency and better engagement. Tilda was thoughtful for a moment. She thought the problem with what I'd just told her was there should be *one* overriding objective—similar to a mission statement—that positioned the organization for continuous improvement.

"You see," she offered, "you can go through the entire process and get to the end of the eighteen-month period and realize other issues that didn't occur to you before, or weren't previously problem areas, have emerged as a result of the changes. The company needs a model that allows for these to be addressed as part of the journey rather than through ad hoc and disruptive change management processes."

I was surprised, to say the least, by Tilda's knowledge of change management principles and was keen to understand how she'd gained her insights. She outlined how every industry and organization has to be prepared for new ways of doing things otherwise, she emphasized, you can miss out on opportunities and, at best, life and work become repetitive and uninteresting. While accelerating the BMW 7 series to an even more alarming speed (we were traveling at well over one hundred miles per hour and reeling in every car in front of us) she asked me to consider film as a prime example of where change has had a significant impact. Tilda explained how her industry had experienced not just technological change, but also many different creative approaches from directors like one of her favorites, Guadagnino. She wanted to know whether I'd seen *I Am Love*. I confessed I hadn't.

"Nick," she said, "it's such a deceptively melodramatic and

somewhat static film. By that, I mean yes, it's a mannered, European love story about deceit and passion, but its telling is so modern and informed by a production design very much influenced by digital technology. If you saw the rushes, Nick, and compared them to the final cut, which has a wonderful golden quality, I think you would understand what I'm getting at."

In a way, even given my limited experience, I understood what Tilda was talking about. Looking over what had been shot at the end of each day on *The Secret Writer*, the product, although well-acted and with a luxuriously appointed set, seemed flat and lacking color. I'd assumed post-production work would enhance the visuals and was interested to know how this would be done. But Tilda wasn't just talking about technology as a standalone issue. She went further and explained the challenges for an actor working in a technology-driven environment. I was again embarrassed to have to answer in the negative when asked if I'd seen *The Lion, the Witch and the Wardrobe*.

"In a film like that," Tilda noted, "you have to fully engage the imagination, even more so than in a nuanced, subtle, and complex story like James'. There are blue screens everywhere. You have one-sided conversations with imaginary creatures while all the time wearing a costume you can hardly move in! I know it's a young person's movie but it was a very demanding experience, especially working with children. So we all need to change, but it's *how* we adapt that's so important."

These were interesting observations that caused me to reflect deeply. It had never occurred to me to think about a creative industry in that way. It was common sense but I'd been so caught up looking at everything through a corporate lens I hadn't realized how much I still had to learn, and from a working environment where, on the face of it, you would never expect to find such a close alignment.

Tilda didn't want to read the entire change management plan (I hadn't expected her to) but she'd be happy to read the executive summary if there was one and provide feedback. I was astonished she would have any interest in the workings of the business world and asked her how a famous actor could ever have acquired such a keen interest in such things. Tilda noted that change affects all of us in different ways and it's important to be prepared for it.

"Anyway," she said, "while removing my Claddagh and putting it on her thumb, my father ran a military bureaucracy for years. He often talked about modernization and the future."

I wanted to ask Tilda about her father. He might have some useful insights. Lessons from the military world, combined with those of the film and corporate sectors, might be interesting. However, without any warning, before I could ask if I could meet him, my red-headed chauffeur steered the car off the main road and into a lane that led up a small hill. It was a beautiful avenue lined with a canopy of large poplars. We emerged into a circular driveway in front of a small castle. The garden was magnificent. There were hedges and shrubs that had been cut into the shapes of animals—a hedgehog, an eagle, and a lion. The massive front door, made from a dark oak-like timber with black iron rivets, opened as if by magic. There was a small woman waiting for us. Tilda embraced her warmly as we crossed the threshold.

There were a great many paintings of the actor in the entrance hall, all of which were very accomplished and, I thought, characterized by a profound sadness. The artist had made her fierce and distant, but had also emphasized her intelligence and emotional depth. They reminded me of Lucien Freud, or even Francis Bacon's early figurative paintings. The only technical fault I could find was what I perceived as a failure to accurately capture Tilda's delicate transparency.

We sat down before an open fire. The hearth was about the same size as my Sydney apartment. The housemaid brought in a tray with tea and scones. There was more to eat than the two of us could possibly manage and Tilda smiled as she told the woman she was far too generous. Tilda drank half a cup of tea. She didn't touch the scones.

Before the housemaid left, Tilda asked her when Sandro would be back. We learned Mr Kopp had left for New York a few days ago for an opening and would be back tomorrow afternoon. Tilda didn't react in any way to this news but asked her to prepare the large guest room for Mr Clement, who would be staying until the morning. Tilda turned her attention to me, flirtatiously twirling my ring around her thumb. She asked me to tell her a little about myself and, in particular, about the ring and who had given it to me.

"I've never seen anything like it," she remarked. "It's not like a normal Claddagh at all—it's too heavy—it feels like it's made from lead."

I told her that while the ring came from a period of my life I preferred to forget, I would share what I could. Tilda walked over to my chair, put her hands on my cheeks and kissed me. She promised I could trust her absolutely.

"Nick," she said, "I sense a bright future. But we must be completely open with each other."

Tilda stood up, walked to the drinks cabinet, and poured two large glasses of Lagavulin.

"Fuck the tea," she laughed, "I think we need something stronger!"

Given Tilda's invitation to reveal more about myself in order to build a stronger connection between us, I took her back to the very beginning and how, as a young man, I had chanced upon an opportunity to manage a group of traveling circus performers. She was shocked when I revealed that two of my colleagues had been killed in an unfortunate accident.

Tilda put her hand on mine. She'd never experienced such a terrible workplace accident but, while noting that a circus posed much greater risks than a film production, advised that safety on major film sets was second to none.

"You see," she explained, "the assets, and by assets I mean the actors I'm afraid, are worth so much the insurance is quite unaffordable if you can't demonstrate you've implemented the right workplace safety measures."

I told Tilda *Circus Mundo* (she loved the name) had been insured but it was for public liability only. Local councils wouldn't let us set up unless we had the right level of cover.

While interested in the work of the trapeze artists, the magicians, and the two lighter-than-air women who could be thrown vast distances in the air, Tilda was particularly intrigued by my description of the two circus strongmen who had been such a driving force over the success and perhaps downfall of the show. I briefly outlined their backgrounds before they became performers—a professional boxer and a former Olympic gymnast. Tilda commented on how incredible it is that people with seemingly unrelated skill sets can bring something different to the arts.

"You're a good example, Nick. You've worked in circus administration and the corporate sector but for some reason you have the necessary skills to be an actor. I don't think your performance could be improved by training. What you have," Tilda offered, "is a gift that can't be taught."

I thanked her for the compliment before she asked me about

the German gymnast who had been a strong influence over the management and strategic direction of the circus. She thought it unusual someone with such a successful sporting background would end up in an Australian traveling show. I agreed, explaining he carried a heavy burden from his time as a professional sportsman and, for that reason, had sought refuge in another country.

"It is quite a sad story," I said. "He'd hoped to come to Australia and forget what he thought was a major professional failure, but he was unable to let go of the past."

She responded that many performers, irrespective of the discipline, carry the weight of the world on their shoulders, and often the only way to be truly alone is to be on stage or in front of the camera.

"You see," she continued with a note of sadness, "performing allows you to lose yourself for a period even if there are hundreds or even thousands of people looking at you. There is a strange but reassuring solitude in such public situations."

Tilda asked about the gymnast's personal difficulties. I explained that Eric had narrowly missed out on the gold medal at the Athens Olympics in the individual still rings event, winning only bronze. It had been a huge disappointment to him and he never got over it. Tilda frowned and grew even paler as I recounted Eric's father's inexcusable behavior after he'd missed out on gold. She stood up suddenly, spilling Lagavulin all over her. The smell of peat was overpowering.

"Nick, you are talking about Eric Strom! I was in the arena

when he lost! It was scandalous because everyone knew his performance was vastly superior to that of Tampakos, who received overly favorable scoring because it was his home Olympics. But Strom didn't win the bronze. No, I am sure of it...third place went to Chechi, the Italian."

It was my turn to be shocked. I told Tilda she was mistaken. I'd come to know Eric very well. He'd shown me his bronze medal. I'd held it in my hands. Tilda said that was impossible and she closed her eyes in order to recall clearly what had happened so many years ago.

"I remember that day very well. My husband and I went to the games because we were both, and still are, big fans of men's gymnastics. I like the girls' events I suppose, and their dexterity and flexibility are extraordinary, but the men have that supreme power and control. Of course, the men look fantastic too! But Nick, there is no way Strom won the bronze. Tampakos, in a workman-like performance, took first place, the Bulgarian Yovchev silver (and some might argue his performance was also worthy of gold), and Chechi, against all expectations given he was coming to the end of his career, took the bronze. There were rumours that Chechi thought Yovchev should have won. But I have it on good authority it was Strom whom Chechi contacted after the games. Chechi told Strom he would have won gold if not for local favoritism. It is entirely possible Chechi gave Strom his medal as a mark of respect."

This very idea had already occurred to me while hearing Tilda's account. I tried to remember handling the medal and whether Eric's name was on it. I had no idea of his last name at the time and anyway the engraving was, I recalled, in the Greek alphabet. Anyway, Tilda produced her phone to prove Eric Strom was not a medal winner but in fact had finished fourth, albeit by a margin of just a few decimal points. Whether the medal belonged to Eric or someone else hardly mattered, but it made me recall my days in the circus with a mixture of terror, sadness, and nostalgia. My thoughts were interrupted by Tilda, who remarked that young female gymnasts who spend the first part of their lives training hours each day become undone by the fact their agility, their elasticity, gradually gives way as they grow.

"It is depressing," she said, "to think that an experienced professional may have no chance against the latest teenage superstar. With the men, Nick, the opposite is true. They start young, like the girls, but they don't develop the required strength until much later. Anyway, in my view the men's events are far more interesting. They are less theatrical and purer if you get my meaning."

I had never thought a great deal about the sport, but I could see what Tilda was getting at. She considered the girls' events to have a greater emphasis on performance whereas the men needed to demonstrate superior strength.

"Anyway, enough of gymnastics and the rights and wrongs of

Athens," Tilda said. "Tell me about the girls flying through the air! Surely it was one of those two who gave you the Claddagh."

"Tilda," I answered, "I'm going to be honest with you. One of the girls in the show, Tama, was my lover, and it was she who gave me the ring. Tama and the rest of the *Circus Mundo* team will always be a part of me but, long before I had the courage to do so, I'd thought many times of escaping what I'd eventually realized was a deceitful, lonely, and overly competitive environment. Of course, I still wonder from time to time what happened to the rest of them, in particular Eric and his partner, Anthony, who I was also close to. They were dangerous but we had, I thought, a close bond. Having said that, I've heard nothing further of *Circus Mundo*. I gave up searching years ago. It just fell off the face of the earth."

Tilda said she understood how I felt about the people I'd worked so closely with.

"The thing is, in the film world, and perhaps this goes for traveling shows too, you develop intimate relationships with your colleagues for brief periods, and then you may never see them again. The funny thing is, I still remember my lines from every production I've been in. For that reason, when I am reminded of a certain scene, I can re-experience the moment as if it were yesterday. I can hear the voices of those I've worked with. It might sound a little strange but I can assure you it's very common amongst actors. One day, Nick, you will experience it too."

I followed Tilda out of the drawing room to the foot of a large circular staircase. She stayed with me in the guest room all afternoon and the rest of the night. She laughed when I said I was in love with her.

I woke to find Tilda sitting at the dressing table brushing her pale orange hair. She asked if I'd slept well and, without waiting for an answer, said I'd have to leave because her husband would be arriving home shortly. I was understandably disappointed by this news but it was even more distressing when she told me it was her husband, the Sandro she'd mentioned the day before, who had painted her portraits. It indicated the deepest type of intimacy—not dissimilar to that of Marx and Asarov.

My first instinct was to point out the shortcomings of her husband's work and how he hadn't quite captured Tilda's peculiar lack of color. I wanted to say the paintings were accomplished but derivative, but thought better of it. The maid knocked on the door and entered without waiting for an invitation. As if unaware of my presence, she announced that the gentleman's car was downstairs. It had somehow been arranged that my driver take me back to Pinewood. I gathered my things and descended the stairs with Tilda who had her arm through mine and was resting her head on my shoulder. I wondered what the future held for us.

When the car came to the end of the avenue of the great house, I saw a flash of orange in the side mirror. It was Tilda, desperately trying to catch up before we turned onto the motorway for the return south. She was laughing, almost hysterically, and nearly tumbled over as she sped down the hill. Tilda was completely out of breath as she fell onto the back of the car. I pushed the button to wind down the glass and Tilda's beaming, translucent face was framed in the open window. "Nick," she panted, barely able to speak, "you need to email me the transition plan! I've changed my mind. We never got around to discussing it so email it to me and we can catch up tomorrow."

Tilda handed me a card with her contact details. I pocketed it and turned around to wave as we turned onto the road, but she was gone.

The drive to Pinewood was not uneventful. We stopped twice. The first time was at a café in Lockerbie. My driver and I had breakfast and coffee. I found out he was studying at the London School of Economics and his father had been a well-known musician. He told me he wanted to work in investment or merchant banking and was hoping to get a graduate position at Standard Chartered the following year. The young man was interested in institutional lending. I told him about my commerce degree and how it had more of a practical focus than economics—which I understood to be more theoretical. He didn't disagree. I explained my studies were more about the practicalities of running a business and general principles of supply and demand.

The second time we stopped we turned off the M6 at Carlisle and had an early lunch at the George and Dragon. The driver asked how I started out in acting. I was tempted to tell him about my background in a corporate advisory firm, but instead said I had successfully auditioned some time ago. He observed how fortunate I was to live in luxury and be driven around in expensive cars. He ungenerously asked, and in a sinister tone, whether I had to cook for myself or did I have someone to do that for me.

It was at this point he mentioned his father. It transpired we were at the George and Dragon because this man's dad, who had long since passed away, had worked there many years ago. He and his brothers were all born in Carlisle. His father, before owning and running a pub in the most god-forsaken town in England, had been in the entertainment industry. He'd played in a number of long-forgotten music groups in the 1970s and had a hit record in 1985 with Alison Moyet, his father having co-written the song *Invisible*. I told him I remembered Moyet from that period but could only vaguely remember that track. He pointed behind me where a gold record was hanging on the wall.

"My dad retired here," he said, "to this pub. He lived upstairs. He was proud of that gold record."

The driver pulled out his wallet and extracted a creased photo of his father with Alison Moyet and the rest of the band. None of them were looking into the camera apart from Moyet who was standing in the center of the group. Their clothing was typical of the mid-1980s with pastel colors and angular patterns. I saw a strong likeness between father and son.

"Sometimes," the young man continued, "people would stop us on the street in Hackney, where we lived in London, and ask my old man for his autograph. Dad liked the attention but there was always a part of him that wondered why the success didn't continue forever. It's ironic isn't it, how my dad was right up there in the industry, and now I'm driving the rich and famous around in fancy cars. The good news is that the council is going to erect a plaque in the middle of the city to celebrate the achievements of Carlisle-born musicians. They've done the same thing in Liverpool opposite the Cavern Club."

I was told that the city council wanted to raise the town's profile and turn it into a cultural hub, but I was barely interested at this stage. I badly wanted to get back in the car and go to Pinewood. I was already missing Tilda and my chauffeur's conversation was irritating. For example, when we got back in the car he asked me what it was like to be famous. I pretended I hadn't heard. Rather than answer such a banal question, one which I was ill-qualified to answer, as we turned off the M6 I commented that the drive hadn't taken nearly as long as I'd expected. He responded that once you get on the motorway it's all plain sailing, especially now the ring roads have all been completed.

We approached the Manor House. James was sitting in the garden reading a copy of *Cinema* magazine. Even from a distance I could see Dustin Hoffman's face on the cover. I thanked the driver and walked over, just as Kate Winslet emerged holding a tray with cheese and biscuits and two negronis. I realized at that moment Tilda still had my Claddagh.

I sensed the driver watching us as he drove away.

Kate handed me one of the drinks. I hadn't expected to see her because of her advertising assignment in France. Before I could ask, James said the weather in Nice had been terrible, the shoot had been canceled, and they'd decided to relax here. We toasted each other although, to be honest, because no-one had said anything about the various romantic attachments that had been struck in recent days, it was a little uncomfortable.

The negroni was delicious—equally sweet and sour and wonderfully refreshing. I congratulated Kate but she said one of the kitchen staff had prepared it. She said they really know what they're doing. Kate asked how I thought *The Secret*

*Writer* was progressing.

"Well Kate," I joked, "if we keep up at this rate the entire production will be finished in a few weeks!"

My co-star observed that when you get the right mix of people on board with a shared vision of what success looks like you can achieve anything. Kate's observation about success resonated strongly with me. It made me realize there was a significant problem with the transition plan, the one I had yet to send to Tilda. I suddenly understood it failed to articulate what success should look like in, say, one year's time or at the end of the eighteen-month transition period. Her observation was eerily similar to Tilda's about the need for a vision statement. While there were plenty of positive initiatives to influence both operations and culture, nowhere did it say concisely and clearly what the desired outcome was.

Given the need for genuine staff buy-in to the change process, it was a crazy oversight from a firm that was regularly awarded large contracts for providing expert advice on business realignment and structural change. The document suddenly struck me as rather pointless and I resolved to advise my Executive Director accordingly. I was, I think, distressed and off-balance because Claire and James had broken up, Claire was now with Elliot, and I was in love with a married woman. I couldn't help feeling things were starting to unravel. I felt rudderless when Daniel was absent from the group.

★

I drank my negroni and excused myself. I was keen to get to know Kate better because she was very approachable and struck me as a very interesting person, but I needed to respond to the Executive Director's invitation to comment on the transition plan while my thoughts were clear in my head. I promised Kate and James I'd be back in half an hour for another of those delicious cocktails.

I was starting to become a little frustrated at the inability of the team in Sydney to come to a final landing on how to move the company in a new direction. I did, however, have to concede I was the one who had stepped away from the process. Perhaps I should have been more grateful for the firm's generosity. I appreciated the Executive Director and the Chief Operating Officer seeing something in me I'd never been aware of—they referred to it as *executive potential.* Perhaps the experience of writing the report had changed me from a reliable but middle of the road employee into someone who was ready to lead.

In any case, I drafted my response to the transition plan and re-read it over and over before I pressed *send.* I was faithful to the original piece of work Claire and I had undertaken and the last thing I wanted to do was undermine the change process. I wanted to be constructive. I also wanted to get Tilda's ideas about preparing an organization for *ongoing* change, you might call it agility, into the mix.

My email stepped out three suggestions. The first was the plan be amended to emphasize building a culture that was equipped to continually change and adapt. The second was that the firm articulate a vision that didn't necessarily describe an end state, but rather a *way of working* or the cultural environment we wanted to create. Finally, I suggested the language be toned down. The plan came across as a little evangelical and I knew that wouldn't work for many of my colleagues. Overall, my email was firm but constructively critical. I felt a considerable weight had been lifted from my shoulders.

When I returned to the garden, Kate was on her own. James had gone to the studio to do some preparatory work for the Gaurige shoot. She asked whether I wanted a negroni.

Kate left me to order more drinks and something to eat. I picked up *Cinema* magazine and turned to the interview with Dustin Hoffman. Hoffman was starring in a new movie by Lars von Trier. It was a *film noir* about human trafficking. Hoffman was playing the lead investigator in an international team of detectives pulled together by Interpol. The team had little chance against a consortium of criminals from Eastern Europe and North Africa that was able to keep moving from place to place at short notice, and had local police in its back pocket.

The article revealed that throughout Hoffman's career he'd always sought roles that would stretch him as an artist. From *The Graduate* through to *Tootsie* and *Rainman* he had chosen characters (or had they chosen him, Hoffman mused) that were so far outside his normal frame of reference he would have to metamorphose. Mainstream Hollywood movies had never really interested him and, contrary to what happens to most actors, his desire to work on alternative projects had only increased. The financial freedom afforded by his success had allowed him to choose projects he was passionate about, often working for vastly reduced fees or nothing at all.

The elder statesman of American acting seemed like an older version of Daniel Day Lewis in that he was very selective about the projects he took on and that he used the *method*. He recounted his preparations for *Tootsie* and how, long before filming had started, he'd dressed as a woman and visited bars to fully comprehend gender complexities. Hoffman explained how the role had a difficulty factor of four because he was an actor playing an actor who was pretending to be a woman who was also an actor. Hoffman moved on to talk about his respect for von Trier.

I didn't make it to the end of the article before Kate re-emerged from the manor house. She was very much looking forward to the Gaurige shoot. She asked whether I had any firm views on the casting. I remarked that her idea of having Daniel, Tilda, her, and me playing different parts at different times would be challenging and questioned whether it might be more sensible to keep it simple so the audience can more easily follow the action. Kate agreed on the face of it that would be the more sensible option but she laughed as she accused me of being too conservative.

I suggested James would need to think very carefully about how to progress the telling of Asarov's novel with, say, both Daniel, and me playing Henry Gaurige. Kate said she would talk to James about it.

I was deflated, but not altogether surprised, when filming resumed and Tilda walked into the studio as if nothing had happened between us. We'd only been apart for a few days but I missed her terribly. While I assumed she would leave her husband, who I found out was not an amateur hobbyist painter but an internationally recognized artist, she was so inscrutable I found it hard to be sure of anything.

Filming took longer than expected. We arrived at the point in *The Secret Writer* where Marx is still working impossibly hard for a man of his age and losing his stamina. He is not well. Aware Marx is fading, Asarov starts to fear for her own writing and that she will never receive the validation necessary for any author. If Marx dies, her future will be quite uncertain. Her response to this uncertainty is to write.

Asarov, after working long days and nights in the service of her tormentor, would retire to her room and write until she fell asleep at her desk. It was there, by candlelight, that the world of the Gaurige Gypsies was born. However, as her narrative developed into one of the greatest stories of all time, poor

Viktoria became so fatigued and despondent she found it difficult to distinguish between the world she had created and her day to day existence.

Her obsessiveness resulted in characters constructed in meticulous detail. Henry Gaurige's mannerisms as he drank coffee took ten pages. The hard and ungenerous face of his son-in-law was afforded a full chapter. She would describe the aroma of the casserole simmering on the open fire, and the sensations of those who experienced it. There was a beautifully crafted passage where the smell of a meal cooked for the extended Gaurige clan caused one of the sons to recall the first days of his life, with a paprika-laden stew boiling in a huge metal iron pot—the same pot, perhaps, I'd seen in my dream. The son saw the pale grey eyes of his mother who, only minutes after the birth, placed him on her breast as she went back to work.

Asarov provided the reader with detail on detail that was as close to painting as it was to writing.

The Pinewood shoot took nearly four weeks. I hadn't understood the complexity of the bridging scenes or how long it would take to film Kate's solo appearances. The latter were surely the most demanding of the entire production. I watched as she revealed Asarov's profound vulnerability, loneliness, and desperation—her descent into a kind of madness. Kate's method was, it seemed to me, to carefully build Viktoria over a number of takes. You might describe it as creating a framework of internal desolation, then using that as the structure for the full characterization. It was the performance of a great artist portraying another.

These were inspirational experiences for me. They prompted me to think again about the process of building a character and how, in certain circumstances and with the right experience, the gap between what is real and what is performance can disappear entirely. I was contemplating these layers of complexity when the director called us together, cast and crew, to inform us we were ready to move on to the Gypsy sequences.

"We will start the day after tomorrow," James said. "However, before we start I have an important and exciting announcement to make. We have secured the services of Alan Rickman to play Henry Gaurige!"

There was a *wrap* party to celebrate the completion of this initial phase of work. Starting again would be like starting a new project, in particular because of Rickman's involvement. Like most people, I knew him from many popular movies over a long career. His laconic acting style would be perfectly suited to the role of Henry, and he was the right age. I suppose they could have artificially aged Daniel, or even me, but Rickman had, James thought, the perfect Gypsy *visage*. Marx, Engels, von Westphalen, and even Asarov could be used for the other Gaurige family roles, but Rickman would provide that strong, central characterization the rest of us could bounce off.

It was at the party that Daniel asked me what I thought of the movie industry. However, rather than answering such a difficult question, one that had so many answers, I asked how he could so easily switch off from Marx. I was interested to understand how, having so profoundly taken on the character, Daniel could shed it and return so quickly to his true self.

"Well," he said, "I have no idea what a true self is! We all play parts in life don't we? We all wear masks, especially around people we are not so close to, and sometimes even around those with whom we are most intimate, and we always take on a role—even if that role is the self! I must admit, though, it was not an easy thing to lose Karl, and I had a similarly difficult time with Abraham Lincoln. Of course, as an artist there are always highs and lows, but I have learned to live with them over the years."

Then Daniel made an interesting comment I have never forgotten. He critiqued my performance, or perhaps it was me. From where he was standing, both as Day Lewis and Marx, he felt my performance was not a *performance* at all.

"It's almost like," he said, "you were Friedrich Engels before you came anywhere near the movie and even before you read the screenplay. In fact, you could say the project has benefited from having the real Engels play himself! Nick, I mean it...as far as I'm concerned, yours is the greatest *supporting* characterization I've ever seen."

I was encouraged by Daniel's description of my acting. While of course I'd made an effort to learn my lines and think carefully about the great German, his role in the story, and how he should interact with the other characters, I'd found it a relatively straightforward process, if a partially involuntary one. From the moment I agreed to audition and do a screen test, I increasingly felt myself disappearing and being replaced by the voice of Engels and James' text. This was what James had been so strongly concerned about—the primacy of the text as opposed to the performance—and finding the right balance between the two.

Before I could respond, Tilda joined us, which was fortunate because Daniel had asked whether I'd got around to reading the books he'd given me. Tilda said she needed to steal me away. She wanted to introduce me to someone. Over her shoulder I thought I saw my chauffeur looking in my direction. When I looked again he was gone.

✷

In fact, there was no-one Tilda wanted me to meet. She wanted to talk to me, not about our relationship as I'd hoped, but about the transition plan. When I sent it to her I never seriously expected her to read it, let alone provide any feedback. Tilda spoke with some urgency, as if something terrible was going to happen if the plan wasn't finalized and implemented as soon as possible. While refilling our glasses with some difficulty from a magnum of Kristal, she said the plan's objectives were admirable but short-sighted. As she'd outlined when discussing the matter in Scotland, she didn't think the plan went far enough in relation to either positioning the workforce for continuous improvement, or providing sufficient support for employees through better use of technology or activity-based working, which she knew was a proven way of getting people to work more collaboratively.

I understood where she was coming from, and appreciated her interest, but I was smarting from what I perceived as a series of personal rejections, strangely combined with moments of intimacy, over the last four weeks. Given my emotionally confused state, my response was defensive.

I answered, perhaps too firmly, that HR wasn't my area of expertise, and that Claire and I had been asked to do an operational review to look for synergies across the teams to drive efficiency and get people out of their silos. I reminded her that business strategy was complex and you couldn't make well-informed decisions without having set foot in the business and talking to the people that worked there. Unusually for me, I revealed a deep level of personal frustration as I suggested activity-based working was an unproven fad that had, I thought, the potential to make a lot of people unhappy by reducing their sense of ownership of the place where they spent such a significant part of their lives. Tilda softened. Her pale green eyes welled up with tears.

"Nick, I'm so sorry for the way I've treated you. My husband and I are open about our relationships so when I was attracted to you I thought nothing of pursuing you. However, the night we were in Scotland, spending time together away from this circus...well it surprised me how strong my feelings are. I know I shouldn't ask you this, because I know it's wrong, but can we spend the night together at my cottage? This last period of filming has been indescribably difficult for me too."

I felt a deep sympathy for Tilda's terrible dilemma, and guilty for having judged her so harshly. We left hurriedly, traveling in separate cars.

My driver commented as I was getting out of the car that he knew I was fucking Tilda Swinton.

I was shocked by this offensive remark and told the driver I wouldn't be needing him again. I recalled the story of his songwriter father. I wondered whether *Invisible*, the song that had made his father a celebrity of sorts, was performed by Yazoo, Moyet's band of the early 1980s, or whether it was a part of her later solo career. As I was walking up the path to Tilda's rented cottage I remembered the song and, incredibly, where I first heard it.

As a teenager, I lived in a small country town where access to the latest music was limited. Our radio and television reception was poor due to the mountainous nature of the landscape so we relied on the local library for magazines and music cassettes. One day, a friend persuaded me to attend a traveling fair which consisted of live performances in the Big Top, rides, fairy floss, and old-fashioned arcade games. We tried the *Dazzler* where you were strapped into a chair that was thrown around in circles. Every few seconds you would feel you were about to crash into another chair hurtling towards you, but at the last second the tracks would steer it away.

We went into the Big Top for a few extra dollars where, even at my age, I could tell we were seeing only half-hearted attempts at entertainment. The performances were no better than you would expect of a group that traveled through Australian country towns, and I recalled wondering where the unusual band of performers came from and what might happen to them. It seemed such a limited profession. In any case, as we were leaving the Big Top, neither of us wanting to stay for the duration of the mediocre show, *Invisible* was playing while a team of teenage girls did a pedestrian acrobatic routine.

I recalled the song word for word. It was about a woman feeling she wasn't getting the attention she deserved. In fact, as I recalled at that moment, standing in front of Tilda Swinton's front door, it was about struggling to understand why you were being treated so poorly by someone you loved and who you thought loved you. But the song went further. The singer was being wilfully ignored, to the extent she felt *invisible*. The song was in no way an appropriate match for the acrobatics, which were intended to be light-hearted but thrilling. *Invisible* was trite and mournful.

Before I could knock on the door of Tilda's cottage she opened it and pulled me inside.

"You're not invisible, Nicholas. I can see you very clearly."

The Executive Director called just after Tilda and I had been discussing the change plan and how to take it further. Tilda conceded some ground and acknowledged she shouldn't have been trying to be such a strong influence over strategic direction. She admitted she'd made unfounded assumptions without having had the benefit of working in the business or being exposed to the culture. She'd provided what feedback she could, and it was now a matter for others to either take it on board or go in a different direction.

The reason the Executive Director had called was not to discuss next steps in the process, but rather to deliver an ultimatum. It wasn't that he was threatening me. That would be unfair. Rather, as he explained, he had a dilemma and it concerned me. It was a problem he hadn't been expecting. In short, he felt he had the team in place to drive the company over the coming period. The Chief Operating Officer would be the principal architect of the transition and the change management executive sponsor. A *change champion*. For too long, he thought, the executive team had made decisions without being closely enough involved in day to day operational matters. He revealed that the intention now was for senior staff to have much greater visibility of their teams and assist *on the ground*.

"And this is my dilemma, Nick. Your insight, and Claire's, has been incredibly useful. You have made a tremendous contribution. However, we need you here and we need a commitment you will return in an executive capacity and become a part of the fabric of the place. Sure, I can accept it's probably for the best that you've been absent for a period because, as with any change process, there have been malcontents who haven't been as ready to adapt to new business models."

The Executive Director didn't want to rush me, but he wanted an answer about my return in the next two weeks. After relaying the conversation to Tilda, she asked what I would do in the longer term and whether I could envisage becoming a full-time actor.

"It seems," she said, "you're going to have to decide one way or the other, and quickly. I'm going to play the lead in a modern western directed by Clint Eastwood. Shooting starts next year, and Clint is always keen to cast a new face. He's a genius at telling local stories with universal themes. You always need another project waiting for you and this could be the one you need to cement your place in the industry."

I was interested in taking on the role of an American and immersing myself in a fictional persona. When I explained this to Tilda she agreed it is a very different task to taking on a real or historical character because it gives you more freedom to improvise. She laughed, as she drifted off to sleep, that I was starting to think like an actor.

We woke early. Tilda was affectionate as we chatted about the prospect of working with Rickman and the wonderful uncertainty of how the Gypsy scenes would play out. Our excitement turned to fear as we walked out the front door of Tilda's cottage. Waiting outside were at least twenty photographers. All were asking questions about our relationship as they pushed cameras into our faces.

Of course, I knew about the paparazzi and how they followed famous people around the world taking intimate photographs without permission and when least expected. Women's magazines were always showing pictures of movie stars at their most vulnerable. Tilda, who no doubt had experience of these situations, told me to say nothing and just get in the car. Terrified, I did what I was told and ignored the chorus of questions, most of which were a variation on *Who are you, Nick Clement?* We were both manhandled, a little roughly at times, but when I made an instinctive move to challenge one of them Tilda stopped me. Her driver was standing beside the car with the rear door open. It was slammed shut as soon as we dived inside. Tilda was laughing as we struggled to sit up.

"Soon you'll be more famous than you ever imagined!"

"But," I argued desperately, "this will be terribly embarrassing. And what about your husband? What will he make of it all?"

I wanted to leave the country immediately. I was beside myself with fear—exposed and humiliated. I blurted out my suspicions about who was responsible—my driver—who had so insensitively made that comment about me and Tilda. She sat up and became serious, asking me about him. I didn't really know a great deal about the man but I recounted what I knew—he was from Carlisle, he was studying economics in order to pursue a career in investment banking, and his father had contributed to the Alison Moyet hit *Invisible*. Tilda's response was unexpected. She said the most successful period of Moyet's career was the least interesting. In her view, even in the last few years and while hardly selling anything, Moyet's work had matured tremendously because it wasn't weighed down by those typically British 1980s pop aesthetics and synthetic sounds.

Tilda's face darkened as she told me what would happen. She would contact her husband and tell him to expect a cheap media story. She would ask her public relations team to put out a statement about how she and I had an early morning rehearsal. I didn't like the approach at all and argued that our relationship shouldn't be reduced to a lie. Tilda held my hand in hers.

"Trust me, I know how to handle these situations, Mr Clement."

Although I'd totally immersed myself in this new world, to such an extent I was now romantically involved with a major international film star, I wasn't prepared for the avalanche of attention that landed on *The Secret Writer*, and in particular, me and Tilda. There were more reporters and photographers outside the Pinewood studio gates. Tilda checked her phone for the latest news. The story had traveled further than she could have imagined. The news sites carried a grainy photograph of Tilda and me in her bedroom. I couldn't work out why the photograph was so unclear. It looked like it had been taken from a long distance away, which was fortunate because Tilda and I were somewhat obscured. Upon closer inspection I realized the photograph had been taken through the curtain of Tilda's bedroom window.

As we drove through the gates, Tilda instructed me to look straight ahead. She started laughing while looking at her phone, reading the headlines from the popular news sites, all of which were accompanied by a slightly different version of the photograph. There must have been three or four different cameras, or perhaps the one photographer had been trying to get a better angle with each shot. The headlines were *Who is Tilda's Mystery Man, Tilda meets her XXX-Man,* and, most alarmingly, *Who Is Nick Clement?* I would now be totally exposed to the world and my colleagues in Sydney. I'd hoped I could keep my adventure a secret until filming was over. Tilda could see I was suffering. She put her arm around me and warned this was part of being in the movie industry.

"I have been lucky," she said, "because my life is banal by industry standards. I've also won a few awards which helps. If you can maintain a level of credibility and not court celebrity in the way some do, and I'm sure you know who I mean, they tend to leave you alone. But it's obvious what happened here. Your driver has, out of jealousy for your situation, the fame, and financial rewards, tried to cut you down."

"That may well be true," I said, "but the last thing I wanted was to reveal what I was doing to the firm back in Sydney. Besides, there is an image of us in an intimate exchange being plastered across the internet! Also, what about your husband? What are we going to do about him? What are *you* going to do about him?"

Tilda waved away my concerns with a tender kiss. She said Sandro already knew everything. After we'd crashed through the media scrum and made our way through the gates, she led me inside the studio complex and said she was looking forward to seeing Alan Rickman.

★

Tilda and I were the last to arrive at the studio because of the delays caused by having to navigate the media. I was relieved to see Claire. She was standing beside Elliot who was talking to Alan Rickman and James in hushed tones. As soon as they saw us they came over. The producer held his arms out in dramatic fashion and hugged us both. Rickman was gracious and serious. He approached us slowly and deliberately, then went down on bended knee, and kissed Tilda on the hand. Rickman offered me his hand and said he'd heard a great deal about me.

Daniel was wearing two giant gold, hooped earrings. His hair seemed to have grown overnight and his heavy beard had been replaced by a rugged-looking goatee. He'd been transformed from a social theorist into a Romani traveler. I sat between Daniel and Kate, the latter laughing as she held up her phone with the photograph of Tilda and me—what she laughingly referred to as our tender embrace.

James called the session to order. He announced the Gaurige filming would take place, after all, in Germany just outside Hamburg. James thanked Claire for organizing the logistics so *The Secret Writer* could be set exactly where Viktoria Asarov imagined it. To my surprise, James announced he was, for the moment, stepping aside as auteur to hand over to Mr Rickman.

Then it was Rickman's turn. He stood in front of the cast

and explained how he and James had agreed that he, as Henry Gaurige, would be the focal point of a series of extended sequences that would, as set out in the script, be interwoven with the story of Asarov. We would be working in ensemble fashion, experimenting with each other's characters. With that short introduction, he handed out new versions of the script. Even on a cursory read through it was clear, Rickman aside, we would be playing multiple roles. I looked at Daniel. His Gypsy earrings were shaking as he leafed through the pages.

James suggested we have a short break before our first improvisation workshop. I'd almost forgotten the paparazzi incident but Tilda reminded me of it by dragging me into her dressing room. I am embarrassed to say that during this hurried encounter I couldn't help but think of the change management plan (or was it a transition plan—it occurred to me the title was crucial to its success) and the job offer. I promised myself I would call the Executive Director in a couple of days. After all, the firm was about to embark on a significant change journey. They'd need certainty around resourcing to ensure it had the best possible chance of success. I felt I'd be missing out whichever decision I made. It's true I had some personal investment in the future of the company. On the other hand, who in their right mind would give up the chance to perform with some of the best in the world?

Tilda, reading my mind and a little breathless, asked what I was going to do. I asked her to stay with me while I called the Executive Director. I'd already made my decision.

In my excitement at having finally made a call on my future, I gave no thought to the time in Sydney. The Executive Director, after answering my call at what I later realized was a time approaching midnight, said he only answered because it was me.

"I thought," he said, "you were running off with Claire for a few months, but I assumed you'd return soon enough. I can hardly believe you'll come back now you're a movie star. Why didn't you tell me all this in the beginning? I would never have had to worry, and you wouldn't have had to string me along."

I could hear his wife asking who was calling at this time of night. He replied, in a whisper, "it's that guy from work I was telling you about who's in a movie with Tilda Swinton."

"Listen," I answered, "I am and will remain committed to the change management project, but now, for obvious reasons, I won't be able to return on a full-time basis, or to Sydney, for an extended period. Having said that, there is no reason I can't act as an external consultant as we roll it out. After all, that's what I've been doing while overseas and, I think, have provided some value. I can assure you I'm not stringing you along, and in fact I'm a little offended considering the amount of effort

I've put into this."

"Nick," he almost shouted, "are you taking the piss? I can't believe you're thinking of combining the roles of actor and business consultant. The two jobs are so different! I think you'd need to guarantee some face to face time as part of the arrangement. If you *are* serious about this you'll need to convince me. I mean, I'm supportive of flexible working arrangements but don't you think this is a little ridiculous?"

"Isn't working digitally," I reminded him, "a key component of the change piece?"

The Executive Director yawned and shouted at the same time, *"Nick, you're an actor for God's sake!"*

The phone went silent for a moment. I thought I'd lost him. When he got back on the line he was suddenly full of energy.

"Listen, Nick, maybe it's not so crazy! Wallace Stevens was an insurance executive. William Carlos Williams was a doctor. They both had normal lives while combining their artistic practice with stable families and normal, executive occupations. Perhaps that type of duality can work for you too! Maybe there is something useful from the acting world that can be applied to the world of business."

I'd never heard of Wallace Stevens or William Carlos Williams. I asked who they were. The Executive Director said that in his view they were the two greatest American poets of the twentieth century.

✴

So, after having initially had such strong reservations about my proposal, he agreed to it. Tilda wasn't surprised. In her view there was no reason to believe I had to give up one profession for another. She agreed that Stevens and Carlos Williams were two examples of how you can excel in more than one field. In fact, without saying what they were, she thought having a balance between the artistic and the everyday could have significant benefits. I decided to explore the two American poets. I'd never read poetry before.

After the excitement of coming to an agreement with the firm, it was time to go back to the rehearsal room. Having the other side of my life sorted out made me feel more centered and I was able to concentrate fully on my acting. Alan Rickman, in the role of director, was both imposing and engaging. He would clap his hands and instantly have everyone's attention. James had a similar skill but his manner was quite different. He came across as a young teacher, whereas Rickman was like a wizened professor of dramatic art.

As Rickman rose to his feet, clapped, and called us to attention, I wondered how James would ensure his vision would not be diluted by another creative voice. I needn't have been concerned. The way James and Alan worked together resulted in a perfect balance between an imagined reality and the very real.

The first session with Alan was extremely challenging. I wasn't sure I'd be able to keep up. No sooner had we done a scene, he would call out *stop*, put his hands on his head, and shout *all change!* He would re-assign the roles (even that of Henry Gaurige to either me or Daniel) and swap Tilda and Kate for Henry's wife. James was darting around with a still camera, taking photographs to help plan the set-up for Germany.

Alan's characterization of Henry was not what I expected. He gave Henry a patriarchal stature I hadn't appreciated from my reading of the script. Alan had a lovely, muffled Germanic/Romani accent. While he gave the dialogue a delicious richness by releasing each word slowly and deliberately, Alan was also able to show so much with simple gestures. Henry commanded his wife, son, or other family member with the slightest eye movement or raising of his brow. There was an imperiousness you wouldn't have thought right for a Gypsy—but it worked. He was the father figure after all, not to mention the inventor of one of the most lucrative ruses in legal history.

Alan's command of the role was emphasized when Daniel or I took over as Henry Gaurige. The scene would become weak and lack focus. The improvisational nature of the performance proved that Henry needed to be that constant presence we could bounce off. Explaining why he needed to step away from Henry from time to time, Alan said he wanted to *see* the performances in a way that would have been impossible working directly with the other actors.

"But make no mistake," Alan explained, "I'm not directing these scenes, just facilitating James' vision! And while I'm at it, can I just say the scope, complexity, and deep humanity of this story is, I think, more than a match for the greatest works of literature. It would be too easy to compare *The Secret Writer* to the great Russian novelists, but I am also reminded of Proust, or even Kafka, because James collapses time and then releases it...or perhaps *expand* is a better word. Does everyone not agree?"

Tilda shot me a look that said, equally, yes this is one of the great stories, and I want to spend the rest of my life with you.

So, by removing himself from the action, Alan was better able to observe the performances. It made sense. Daniel was the only one who didn't seem convinced or sure of himself. It may have been because he didn't have the *one* role to transform himself into. Recognizing his discomfort, I asked him out for dinner. Tilda wanted to come too. She recommended a Viennese restaurant not far from Pinewood.

★

Daniel was happy to be invited. He seemed relieved as he said there was nothing he'd rather do than sit down to a quiet dinner with two of his dearest colleagues. So, that evening, we drove to *Der Wiener* restaurant, on a narrow country road just off the motorway. It looked like a ski chalet. There were red and white checked curtains, matching tablecloths, and the signage was in gothic lettering. The wait staff wore dirndls and lederhosen and the *maitre d'hotel* wore a bow tie and braces.

Given we were the only customers, the number of staff seemed preposterous. It was hard to imagine anyone finding the restaurant, and even then they may have been turned away by the clichéd presentation. The waitresses and *maitre d'* fussed efficiently over us all evening. We were hungry after a long day's work and ordered two large salads—broccoli and cucumber, and potato. Tilda ordered an Austrian Riesling-style wine while we turned our minds to the main courses.

I ordered the jäger schnitzel, as did Daniel. Tilda ordered chicken soup and homemade noodles. The wine was superb. The salads appeared in enormous bowls alongside our mains. They were the largest restaurant servings I'd ever seen—dwarfing the tiny portions we were given at *L'Arpege*. The veal was covered in a rich cream and mushroom sauce with a side of fried potatoes. I thought Tilda would never manage all her broth but to my surprise finished it before Daniel and I were even half way through our veal.

We were silent for a time. There was a light-hearted brass band playing over the speakers. Tilda was the first to speak as she picked at the cucumber.

"So, Daniel," she said in a way that seemed to be teasing rather than genuinely inquisitive, "how are you finding the James McNeil-Alan Rickman experience? We've never really discussed the project in detail and I must say, apart from the first few days, you seem to have lost a little confidence. James spent some time with you early on and I've wanted to know for some time what it was he said. You seemed rather troubled."

Daniel looked like he'd aged greatly as he reached across the table and placed a hand on each of our shoulders. He squeezed so hard I nearly cried out in pain.

"I see," Daniel said. "You want to explore how I'm managing in an unfamiliar acting environment. Don't misunderstand me, I'm familiar with acting! But it must be obvious to all but the most imperceptive I have landed in a project that's quite different to anything else I've done. I feel I've lost something of myself."

Daniel's eyes were welling up with tears. It was an incredibly touching moment. We were seeing the naked Daniel Day Lewis for the first time. All his characters were put to one side as he sat across from us, picking at his potatoes like a child. The mushroom and cream sauce had started to solidify.

"You are two intelligent and thoughtful people," he said. "You must have noticed at times during *The Secret Writer* I have been unsure of myself—a little lost."

I remarked how I'd noticed a change in his outlook since the first day of rehearsal. In no way did I want to upset him, but

I told him that in his few moments of vulnerability, when he had for a second lost his characterization, I had been struck by the lack of anything, or anyone, behind it. I immediately regretted saying this (and in hindsight it was a presumptuous and cruel remark) because Daniel broke down in tears. It took him some time to pull himself together. He blew his nose on a red and white serviette and talked about his childhood and teenage years. He explained how difficult it was for him to choose acting over cabinet making.

"I was lost and needed direction. My father was a pain in the arse and I didn't want to turn into him. I was offered a place in drama school and things just took off from there. It was an accident more than anything. But Nick, how perceptive you are! You see I use acting to escape having no sense of myself. I clothe myself in the lines of others, but lose all sense of relevance when the project is not purely about the character I am playing. I feel so absent from the world."

Daniel must have reached a point in his life where he needed to unburden himself. Perhaps he was telling the truth for the first time. Daniel's life was crashing down around him but when I glanced at Tilda she seemed to be stifling laughter.

"Can *you* tell *me*," he asked, "how you feel when you are deep inside the character? I make a scaffold—clothes, mannerisms, a voice—and gradually bring the pieces together until I have something whole and in which I can live. But I want to know what it's like for others."

I said I was too inexperienced to have a view but Daniel cut me off, impatiently telling me to give him a straight answer.

"Dan," I said, "I'm a beginner but I'll try to explain. For my audition, I had to learn the lines by heart, and it was through that process I came to *know* the text. But I had the benefit of having some idea of James' intentions for the movie. Anyway, at some point I found myself in a state of transition. I was neither me *nor* Friedrich Engels. I was in a daydream where the words were lifted from the page so they could enter my physical being. I think the simple act of repetition had a profound effect by imprinting Engels onto me. Like a tattoo almost. Does that make any sense at all?"

Daniel nodded. He asked me to continue as he took a large gulp from his glass of Riesling, clumsily spilling some onto his drawstring shirt.

"I'm not sure how to put it," I said. "I feel like I don't yet have the acting vocabulary to explain what happens to me when performing. But I'll tell you this. When I've dissolved into character, I completely lose myself. It isn't a conscious process, and certainly not something I can switch on and off while inhabiting that space. Rather, my *understanding* of the transposition only occurs to me *after* the performance. When I am back to being me."

The great actor wanted to know if I carried the character around with me when I wasn't on set. That is, whether I had become Friedrich Engels to such an extent I couldn't part with him.

"No, not at all, I can return to myself without thinking about it. After all, we are just pretending are we not?"

Daniel explained his approach in a way that touched me deeply.

"I hear you, my friend, but I'm different. Unlike your time-limited transformation, I become so absorbed in the role it can take months for me to return to normal. The problem is, when the character has been shed I feel like I've shaved another part of me away. Over the years, the intensity of this sensation has increased with every role I've taken on. Now, having had to give Marx up, I feel dreadfully exposed. It's as if people can see right through me and understand that, in fact, I am nothing. This feeling of aloneness, of transparency, has always been mitigated by owning the entire film project—one where I play the title role, am in every scene, and the work is of such intensity I can leave the vacuum of my real existence behind. It occurs to me that that is why I am so good at acting and why I win so many awards. I have more awards than I know what to do with! They come in such strange shapes and sizes it's almost impossible to store or display them in a tasteful way. But I digress. I have come to believe, and perhaps the realization has been brought about by my experience with you, Nick, that my acting ability is inversely proportionate to my substance as a human being. That is, I am nothing, and as a result of this my acting is of the highest quality. Noone understands the horror of my situation. Even after the movie is over and I go to Los Angeles, New York, London, or Paris to promote the film and explain what it was like playing a particular character, what it was like working with the director...well that just becomes another version of me that is not, in fact, me. Or perhaps it is me! I'm always so confused but at the end of the day, or project, I feel that any part of the real Daniel Day Lewis has been sublimated or destroyed by my performance."

I thought carefully about Daniel's revelations. I always had in the back of my mind James' notion that building a character was not about constructing something *real,* but rather creating a *voice.* It was time to bring Tilda into the conversation who I hoped could say something based on her own considerable experience that would relieve Daniel of his desperation. However, when I asked her for her thoughts she was asleep and obviously had been for some time.

"Nick," Daniel said, "don't worry about Tilda or any of what we've discussed. I must say it's been a supreme pleasure to talk frankly with such a gifted artist. Just wait until we get to Germany—I have a big surprise for everyone. I promise you won't be disappointed!"

✶

I gently woke Tilda while Daniel paid the bill. The *maitre d'* was obviously pleased with whatever gratuity Daniel had left. He bowed his head in appreciation, clicked his heels in the military style then hurried to the door to open it for us. Daniel asked if we could drop him at Pinewood as he had work to do. Tilda was smoking a cigarette and Daniel and I each took one. The car quickly filled up with smoke. The cigarette was strong, with an old-fashioned, smooth Virginian flavor.

Daniel got out of the car without saying a word. Thick streams of blue-grey smoke shot out from his nostrils as he marched towards the studio. I wondered what he could be doing there at that time of night. There was considerable activity, as usual, from other projects, but no-one from *The Secret Writer* would be there. As we continued on to Tilda's, she commented on the meal.

"People don't often associate the Germanic peoples with high quality cuisine," she said, "but I disagree. There is a surprising delicacy, not to mention love, in Austrian-German food that other countries simply can't match. The Latinos come close—there is a wonderful rustic quality to much of their cooking. But for me, I'll take a well-made Austrian noodle soup every time. I know you won't believe me, Nick, but I also love the way they prepare the veal. They beat it so thin it's like a wafer."

It was indeed a most tender piece of meat. I described my initial concern that the mushroom and cream sauce would overwhelm the meat but how, in fact, it turned out to be very well balanced.

"Yes," Tilda replied, "*balance* is precisely the right word. And the Riesling, Nick, was it not like nectar?"

I agreed and suggested we eat at *Der Wiener* again. Tilda reminded me we would soon be in Germany and there would surely be plenty of opportunities to savor Teutonic cuisine. She was right. We had a day or two more of improvisation and then we would be off to Hamburg. Claire would already be there taking care of the setup. I asked Tilda what she made of Daniel's revelations.

"Nick, let's have a whiskey."

Tilda poured two generous tumblers of Laphroaig and sat opposite me across the glass-topped coffee table. We raised our glasses and drank, Tilda contemplating the amber fluid. She wasn't totally dismissive of Daniel's performance at the restaurantbut she came close.

"My dear Nick, I was exhausted but still caught a little of the usual drama actors like to create to add substance to their lives. You shouldn't concern yourself too much with Day Lewis. As you may have noticed, his approach to acting is very intense, almost to the point of being ridiculous, but it's no better than any other. You see, actors like him, a Dustin Hoffman, or a Sean Penn, are obsessed with *living* the character—you know what I mean, Nick, and we have discussed it often enough. They have this fascination with acting as an art form when of course it's no such thing. The misapprehension that acting has anything to do with art is a problem for our industry and will one day destroy it. How can I explain it? Let me see...Mark Rothko is an artist, Leonardo da Vinci, John Cage, Stravinski, Picasso...they are artists. They investigate and create new worlds in an original way. They are somehow able to pull magic from the air, tie it together, and make a representation that is new, other-worldly, but somehow deeply human. They produce work that is based on a profound haecceity. A certain *thisness!* I'm just not sure that method acting can match that sort of achievement and I doubt its validity anyway. If you look at the history of acting and performance more broadly, the notion of actor as artist only emerged about a century ago. In fact, a hundred years ago society considered female actors as little more than prostitutes!"

Tilda was just getting started and downed the rest of her whiskey.

"Nick, you need to understand there are two main reasons actors need to consider themselves artists. The first is that acting has become a very well-paid profession. In the first part of the century, cinema gradually, and then quickly, took over from vaudeville and theatre as the preferred form of entertainment. The technology allowed thousands of simultaneous performances around the world and generated millions. Producers, directors, and actors all became impossibly wealthy. It's hard to justify such a privileged existence without there being a serious foundation to the profession. So, Stanislavski and Strasberg came to the rescue by applying the thickest layer of theory over the top of acting.

How can we justify these crazy lives we lead? We not only call actors artists but we make it into a *high art* form. The second factor is equally important but a little more complex. From the early twentieth century we've gradually seen the development of the importance of *self* in all walks of life. Recording devices, gramophones, music cassettes, and now social media have provided us all with the ability to hear and express ourselves when and wherever we like. Everything today is about me, what *I* think, and what *I* see—the world as it rotates around the individual. In this context it's important for everyone, and for none more so than actors whose profession is now called high art, to think of themselves as creative and artistic and as producers of *content*. Combined with the need to justify our privileged lives, we call ourselves artists and blow the self up to the grandest proportions. But, my darling, it's just pretending! On the other hand, take our young director. Now *there* is an example of a true auteur who has imagined an impossible new world and is realizing it with the help of a few actors. In my view, his is the artistic vision we should be applauding."

As the week unfolded I reflected on what Tilda had said about Daniel Day Lewis and the acting profession. I observed my fellow actors and noted the subtle differences in approach. For example, Alan Rickman's work was a real *performance*.

You might say he owned the space around him. Like all great actors, he became a focal point, not just for the action, because after all he was playing the central figure in the Gaurige part of the film, but for the eye. I couldn't help but be drawn to him when watching from the sidelines. He became larger when he was acting, and more physically imposing, somehow dwarfing his colleagues. Having said that, there was a subtlety and stillness I also found very appealing.

Kate's acting was studied, light-hearted, and versatile. She was able to inhabit Asarov while playing any of the Gypsy women. It was a complex assignment. She could be talking with Henry or arguing with Jenna Gaurige (Henry's eldest son's wife, generally played by Tilda) but at the same time needed to show enough of the novelist to demonstrate these Gypsies were, after all, her imagination. To this day it remains unclear to me how she was able to achieve this duality.

I couldn't, in all honesty, make an objective assessment of Tilda's acting. I was in love with her and found her intoxicating. With Daniel, no matter which part he was allocated, he stepped into it quickly and expertly. Even in rehearsals he looked exactly like a Gypsy and had started to look less and less like Daniel every day. He was shedding his skin yet again, while clothing himself in another.

After the long series of complex and challenging rehearsals, during which James and Alan had worked out how to realize the vision of a story within a story within a story and enable all of them to interweave through the conceit of Viktoria Asarov's imagination, James announced filming would start in Hamburg the next day.

"On to the wrap party! Thank you, Mr Elliot!"

Elliot had organized the event at Pinewood Manor House. Over the last few weeks I hadn't spent much time there. Tilda and I had taken to staying at her cottage. The party was attended by all the cast and crew, with the notable exception of Daniel. I was told he'd gone ahead to Hamburg.

Unfortunately, my evening was continually interrupted by my phone, alerting me to emails and missed calls from the Executive Director. The constant requests for contact were becoming tiresome. Eventually, interrupting an interesting conversation with the director of photography about early post-war filmmaking and the rise of 1950s English comedy, I went to the apartment and returned the call. The Executive Director was relieved to hear from me. I could hardly get a word in as he described the staff discontent at what were perceived to be the summary dismissals of Steve and Jaime, and a series of disastrous staff engagement sessions that had been contracted out to a third party. The decision to go external had been taken because the firm wanted an objective approach to consultation. The executive team thought any internally-run process would be viewed as tokenistic. The problem was the use of an independent company had been taken as patronizing.

If the situation wasn't managed carefully, he warned, the entire change process would be derailed.

I could hear the pain in his voice, but I just wanted to go back to the party and learn more about Peter Sellers and the creation of Ealing Studios and Rank Pictures. Finally, in an effort to placate him, I said going with an external provider to lead the engagement process was risky because, as the Executive Director had suggested, it could easily come across as *lip service* if it wasn't expertly managed. I recommended an all-staff forum to clear the air, and that the executive nominate individual team members to lead the consultation. My suggestion calmed him down. The Executive Director said he should have thought of that himself, or at least, he wondered out loud, "The new Chief Operating Officer should have come up with something. *That's why she was hired!*"

I had to accept some of the blame for the external consultant. It had been my idea in the original draft of the review report, and there was no escaping that fact.

"It's not anyone's fault," I said, "that the consultation didn't go well—apart from perhaps the company contracted to undertake it. Listen, just identify some key non-executive staff who have potential and are enthusiastic about the new direction and task *them* with leading the staff engagement."

Although I hadn't thought a great deal about it, and was speaking off the cuff, I thought it a good approach, if not without its own risks. You would have to be careful to choose the right people, but if you did the results could be spectacular.

I signed off by saying I may not be contactable for at least the next few weeks because we were relocating the shoot. The Executive Director thanked me for being available. He'd provide further updates as necessary. I could feel my enthusiasm for the project waning. The firm's clumsy approach to reform and cultural change was preventing it from moving forward. I couldn't help thinking I could have done a lot more if I'd been back in Sydney.

I returned to the party and quickly resumed my conversation with the director of photography. He hadn't moved from his position beside the punch table.

"You see," he continued, as if our conversation hadn't been interrupted, "life in Britain, and London in particular, had been miserable for more than thirty years. There was the Great War, the depression, the threat of another war with Germany, and then the war itself. Imagine what it was like to live through the Blitz and food rationing. Children were sent off to the north. After the horrors of the first half of the century, England found itself full of hope and in the midst of economic prosperity. It was at the heart of world power. At the same time, there was a nostalgia or sentimentality for English traditions and a refreshing willingness after so many years of pain to have a good laugh, often at our own expense. A new, vibrant group of entertainers hit radio, then film and television, many of whom had learned or honed their craft during the war either as amateur entertainers or through learning to laugh in the face of extreme adversity. The end of the war and our pivotal role in victory gave us a strong patriotic fervor and a new perspective on life after decades of hardship. It was an opportunity to celebrate Englishness and reveal it in a way that had never happened before. Almost for the first time, our cockneys, Liverpudlians, Mancunians, Novocastrians, and even our West country farmers with their quaint country ways were raised up as heroes of the national identity. Sellers, Milligan, Guiness, Sid James, and others too numerous to mention captivated the spirit of the country and gave us the opportunity to hear and see ourselves. It was a hugely successful period, even if some of the movies were steeped in nostalgia."

The cinematographer kindly offered to lend me some DVDs of a period in English cinema that obviously meant a lot to him. I thanked him. Just as the conversation was coming to an end, I noticed Sandro Kopp standing on the other side of the room.

Tilda was by Kopp's side, apparently unconcerned at the prospect of an awkward meeting. Her husband raised a glass of champagne, toasted me from a distance, and threw his heavily bearded head back, laughing. Inexplicably, Tilda put her arms around him in a drunken, carefree embrace. Kopp was handsome. He looked like a rugged German mountaineer. They made a beautiful couple.

It was one of those excruciating moments when I wanted to be alone in my own misery but couldn't find the space to escape. Nor did I want to draw attention to myself. The room was full to capacity. The noise was overwhelming. I realized the big band music was, in fact, coming from a live band. It was playing a stripped back version of *Chattanooga Choo Choo*. I made my escape to the garden. I needed fresh air and a drink, and as I took one from a tray I stumbled onto the grass where people had gathered in small groups. I was disconsolate. I couldn't understand why Tilda had invited her husband. Our relationship was, I'd believed, passionate and profound. I'd assumed they would separate so Tilda and I could move on with our lives together.

Kopp suddenly appeared before me, smiling and holding out his hand. His German accent was not dissimilar to the one Daniel had employed when playing Karl Marx.

"I'm Sandro," he said. "Tilda has told me a great deal about you. I feel I know you already. I would very much like to explore your ideas on acting and organizational design. Tilda tells me you have a unique approach to both."

Sandro nodded to a cast iron garden table and chairs which might have been put there just so we could sit down and talk. He took a magnum of champagne and two glasses from a passing waiter.

"Nick," Sandro said, making himself comfortable while leaning across the table so as to concentrate fully on me, "I am setting up a gallery in New York. It will be a significant venture and will represent only the greatest modern painters. I need to build an organizational structure that is both flexible and creative. I also desperately want to paint your portrait."

I asked Kopp why he wanted to paint me.

"Actors are interesting people," he answered. "They change from one moment to the next and their real selves can go missing for weeks on end. I speak from personal experience. Nick, you have seen my portraits of Tilda. What I am trying to do is capture the moment inside the actor—that moment when the real self is revealed! It is a difficult thing to achieve, but I think I have managed to perfect it with her. Now I would like to capture the Nick Clement who is stripped of the shroud that is the actor's false or imagined self. In my opinion, actors are fragile, or brittle, because they are never quite sure of who they are. It's as if they might break at any moment and that's what I tried to capture in Tilda. My paintings, I hope, give a sense of her in her still moments, just before she becomes something else—or perhaps I should say *someone* else?"

It was the strangest feeling to feel so comfortable in the presence of my competitor. Kopp was pensive as he described Tilda in a way that demonstrated a close emotional attachment.

"Nick, Tilda is not only *characterized* by her stillness, a feature that is obvious to everyone. No, Tilda *inhabits* stillness, and lives, and acts, through a lack of movement. You see, this is what makes her performances so revelatory. Every expression or smallest movement comes as a surprise because it emerges from her glacier-like visage. I believe this is what makes her performances so engaging and so different to any other artist. And you know, I think you have it too. You're no actor, and that is what makes your Friedrich Engels a standout characterization. I'm sure that's why Tilda has fallen for you."

Sandro Kopp stood up and left the party. I couldn't help but feel sorry for both of us.

I woke up as if in a desert. My eyes hurt. I remembered we were flying to Hamburg that morning when Tilda arrived in her car to pick me up.

"Tilda," I said on getting into the car, "I met Sandro last night. Why did you invite him? It could have been disastrous."

The actor, with a cigarette in her mouth and her eyes on the passing landscape, denied she'd invited anyone.

"But you have to admit he's rather charming. I'd be surprised if he hadn't offered to paint your portrait. He likes to work with interesting people. There is something about the way he paints me that makes me think I'm seeing myself for the first time. On the other hand, it confirms for me who I am."

Tilda described how Sandro had painted Robert de Niro at

his ranch in Colorado Springs. Sandro placed him against an epic backdrop of water falling rapidly through a deep ravine.

"However," Tilda concluded with a sigh, "sometimes the most interesting ideas don't translate into the best results. Sandro, for reasons known only to him, made De Niro's face too angular and the background, with the drama of the waterfall, was what caught the eye, not the intended subject! It was an awkward moment, and I don't think Bob looked at Sandro in the same way again."

It was an interesting anecdote. We approached the airport and, while I was excited to be going to Germany for the first time, I was jealous of Sandro and his ability to capture Tilda's essence.

The flight to Hamburg was brief. Tilda rested her head on my shoulder and slept. I overheard James and Alan talking about the shoot. Alan was concerned this next phase could be challenging, even for experienced actors. James wondered whether I would be able to handle the pressure. Alan dismissed his concerns.

"James," Alan said, "did you not see Nick's efforts in rehearsal? It's like he's been acting all his life. While his style is more European than the rest of us, with the possible exception of Tilda (who can do anything), he is able to perform *around* his colleagues like no-one I've ever seen. Have you ever noticed, and you must have seen it in the rushes, your attention is drawn most to Nick when he isn't speaking or when his character is just a presence? He has an uncanny ability to fill the *performance* space while allowing his fellow actors to shine."

James said I was like Alain Delon, the French actor. Alan laughed loudly in that restrained style of his.

"Yes, I see what you mean—not quite at that level but you never know! Delon's method was so laid back he was barely acting at all. Now there's an actor who understands, as you have described it to me, the importance of being a vehicle for the text. Delon just says the words and allows the drama to take its course."

We arrived in Hamburg and were whisked through customs. We climbed into a black minibus with tinted windows. Rather than staying in the city and commuting every day to our location, we would be staying in the Sachsenwald Forest in custom-built cabins. As we entered the woods, even though in the middle of the day, it became dark and atmospheric, the light being cut out by giant spruce, fir, and elm trees. It was one of the most beautiful places I'd ever seen.

✶

We emerged from our minibus to be greeted by Claire. She'd been in Hamburg and the Sachsenwald for some time making sure everything was ready for our arrival. Claire took us into a part of the forest where sunlight was almost completely lost to the dark green canopy. She showed us to our accommodation. There was an *Alan Rickman* sign hanging on the door of the first cabin, the gothic letters burnt into a timber panel. The cabin was surprisingly large. It had a small but modern kitchen and a generous double bedroom with a study area, desk, and computer. We left Alan to settle in while Claire showed me, Kate, Tilda, and James to our own cabins, each with our name hanging on the door. Daniel was absent but Claire said he'd join us later.

There was a barbeque lunch. We were led to a large open campfire kitchen where bratwürst were being served with sauerkraut, mustard, and tiny bread rolls. There was an enormous cast iron pot filled with chicken soup. The rest of the day was spent eating, drinking, and chatting with the crew. I spent time talking to the costume designer, Anna, who promised I would very much like the Gypsy outfits. She explained to me her dilemma.

"You see," Anna said, "I needed to find a balance between a truly authentic costume and making the actors comfortable. It's often a challenge to replicate clothing so it looks authentic while ensuring the performers can concentrate on their acting. The last thing I want is Tilda Swinton complaining about the outfits!"

I was interested in the challenges facing a costume designer and would have liked to hear more. However, I noticed a plume of purple-grey smoke above the tree canopy, the source of which was some distance away. I asked Anna what it might be but she had no idea. Others noticed the smoke too. A group of us started walking through the forest in search of its source. Tilda, Kate, Anna, James, Claire, some of the crew, and I pushed our way through a thicket of ferns and came upon another, smaller clearing. I was amazed by what I saw.

The first thing that struck me was the Gypsy caravan. It was purple, red, green, and white, but the colors were muted, aged by the weather, and looked hundreds of years old. Behind the caravan was a grey draught horse that also belonged to another century. The campfire, from which the trail of smoke rose gently into the air, was heating a black pot sitting precariously on the coals. The man sitting beside the fire was on his haunches stirring it with a long, wooden spoon. He had shoulder length hair tied in a ponytail and was wearing a brightly colored waistcoat over a cream linen blouse. It was like we had happened upon a moment that had been frozen in time, or a painting by Buttersack, the only movement being the gentle rustling of leaves and the horse's nostrils brushing against the ground. We looked at one another uneasily because we were, I think, unsure whether to retreat or to inquire who this man was and whether he needed any assistance.

A pile of papers on the ground, a document of some kind, caught my eye. It was the only clue that I had not unwittingly traveled back in time. I took a few steps forward and saw that the document was, incredibly, the screenplay of *The Secret Writer.*

I called out, a little afraid, "*Is that you?*"

The man stood up slowly, as if scarred by the history of all mankind. He was holding a clay pipe in his left hand. The burning tobacco, if it was tobacco, smelled like death. It was the great actor, Daniel Day Lewis. He greeted us with a broad smile.

"I was just going through the screenplay," he said, "and I must say these Gypsy scenes are filled with the most damnedly beautiful writing. It is so nice to see you all. Do you like the caravan? I've spent so many weeks building it. Perhaps we can use it as one of the props for the movie?"

I hardly knew what to say in the face of this incredible and alarming metamorphosis. I shouldn't have been surprised because I'd already witnessed Daniel become someone else. However his Karl Marx was a transformation largely through voice, movement, and costume. Daniel's effort this time was overwhelmingly physical. While Marx was a relatively old man, the Gypsy before me was a youngish but weather-beaten fellow. His shirt, waistcoat, and trousers looked like they'd never been washed. I was repulsed by the body odor of someone who hadn't bathed in weeks.

"Daniel," I asked, "how in hell did you manage to build this caravan?!"

The others in the group, Tilda and Anna included, touched it as if it wasn't real. They pointed out details like the intricate fleur de lys carvings and the faded mustard color of the rear door.

"It's a long story, but a good one," Daniel promised. "You may recall that at *L'Arpege* I mentioned I was planning to sail across the Irish Sea. When *The Secret Writer* came along I must admit I was tempted to ask for a delayed commencement because I was keen to finish the boat and keep a promise I made to myself. At some point in the construction of my twelfth-century replica of the kind of vessel used to travel to the west coast of Britain for trading and other purposes, my attention became focused on the construction of a Gypsy caravan. My research revealed that Gypsies rarely bought their caravans from those who sold buggies and the like to farmers and the middle classes. Rather, they would either fashion the caravans from timber they found or stole, or adapt them from carriages they managed to separate from their owners. They never bought anything! I made arrangements to transfer my home workshop to a vacant storage area at Pinewood. I spent every spare moment building it based on illustrations and drawings a friend at the National Library dug out for me. I had the thing transported to the north Sachsenwald yesterday and then drove it to where you find me now. I must say, I very much like the idea of the cabins, and I apologize for not making use of mine, but I would prefer to stay here with Daisy. For the duration of the Gaurige shoot I want to be a Gypsy and live like one. It's very pleasant in the open air! Would anyone like to see inside the caravan? I decorated it myself although I confess I didn't make the furniture. I didn't have time. In the manner of the Romani people I used found objects to recreate the interior based on what I could glean from my research. There is so much information, but hardly any seems definitive. These people are quite a mystery!"

As Daniel stood up he assumed yet another new dimension. He'd been a middle-aged man, aging gracefully in the way the famous do, and then overnight had become an elderly German obsessed with class structures, economic theory, and the ever-expanding industrialization of Europe. Now, at this moment, everything about him said the Gypsy before us had been on the earth for centuries.

"By the way," he said, talking to Anna who had commented on the fleur de lys design on the caravan, "it's not a fleur de lys but I can see how you made the mistake. The symbol *you* are referring to is a French royal symbol dating back to the earliest Gallic principalities. It's a stylized version of the lily and symbolizes status and nobility. The symbol on the side of the caravan is in fact a *kalinna.* Its origins are unclear, and while the literature is inconclusive, it most likely was born in India several thousand years ago where it is thought the Romani people originally emerged before making their way to Europe, settling in the eastern part of the continent, and then, as we all know, traversing the globe. The great Romani diaspora. To be honest, I don't know, and I don't think anyone does, whether the *kalinna* is a religious symbol or just purely decorative, but I agree it does look a lot like an upside-down fleur de lys. It's even possible," Daniel suggested, "the *kalinna* was used as the prototype. Anyway, they are both beautiful."

I was pleased to see him again, and to find him so content, but as at Pinewood, Daniel remained strangely apart from the group for the duration of the shoot. It was either a supreme version of professionalism or a profound loneliness. Tilda distracted me from my thoughts by tugging my arm, rolling her eyes, and suggesting we go to her cabin for a drink and an early night before shooting started the next day.

By the time we got inside it was nearly five o'clock in the evening and already almost dark. Tilda reached into the small refrigerator and extracted a bottle of champagne. Two champagne flutes appeared. Before Tilda had poured the wine we were interrupted by a knock at the door. It was one of James' assistants. The young man was carrying a large flat package wrapped in a number of layers of brown paper and protective plastic. It was heavy. Tilda was annoyed by the interruption, but when she saw the package she became excited.

"Nick, open it straight away. But be careful—it might be fragile."

I peeled away the layers of bubble wrap, careful not to damage whatever was inside. There were at least ten layers of brown paper, each of which I passed to Tilda who folded them and placed them neatly on the floor. I was overwhelmed by what I found. Sandro Kopp had sent his portrait of me to the Sachsenwald forest. It was in a black wooden frame that looked handmade. He'd painted my head and shoulders against a backdrop that looked not unlike that of the Mona Lisa—a heavenly but desolate wasteland. I felt like it was the first time I'd seen myself. Tilda had a similar reaction.

"Nick, do you see what Sandro's done? He's reflected you as a balancing force in the world. Or perhaps force is the wrong word. *Presence* is better. Yes, you provide balance and perspective while maintaining a distance from all that happens around you."

"It's interesting," I responded, "I've never seen myself represented artistically. It's rather unsettling because I feel like someone has looked deep inside me and reflected outwardly what should perhaps be kept silent. But he's good. I will admit he's captured something...what it is I can't quite be clear on but it's definitely me!"

Tilda reached across and touched the cheek on the head of the portrait with the back of her hand.

"He's not quite got the color of your skin," she laughed. "He's given you a slight tan!"

The morning call was for four o'clock. We ate salami and bread rolls before being ushered away to makeshift dressing and makeup rooms. I was given a short beard. Tilda and Kate were wearing head scarves. Alan and I were dressed in a way that was not dissimilar to the outfit Daniel had chosen.

For the domestic Marx scenes shot at Pinewood, nearly all the filming had been conducted from three cameras which for the most part were static. That is, everything was set up to enable close ups or shooting from pre-arranged angles. The cameras only moved short distances on their tracks. Here, in the forest, the director of photography was issuing instructions to two cameramen positioned in and around the actors. James gave a brief introduction that picked up on his and Alan's ideas about movement.

"Forget about the cameras!" James implored us. "Pretend they're not there. They'll be close to you, in your face, from behind, and in front, but just forget you're in a movie."

The filming would be done in a series of simultaneous, long-shot sequences. Alan echoed James and encouraged us to be as free with our movement as possible.

"We're Gypsies after all!" he exclaimed, clapping his hands and laughing.

We were about to shoot a long scene—the celebration of the return of one of the Gaurige sons who had, after seven years, managed to secure ownership of a significant landholding in another principality. The son, played by Daniel, had returned with his wife and three young children. The scene required the presence of a large Gypsy entourage. There were a great many extras. I heard Tilda's voice. She approached one of the extras, a particularly tall man, and almost shouted with delight.

"You're Eric Strom, the Olympic gymnast, are you not?!"

There was no mistaking the large man dressed as a Gypsy was Eric, one of the two strongmen I'd worked with years ago in *Circus Mundo*. Tilda was excited to meet him. She introduced herself.

"Of course, you already know Nick."

She remarked at the extraordinary coincidence that we'd been reunited so far from Australia—and in such bizarre circumstances. We shook hands. Tilda blurted out it had been a travesty Eric had been denied the gold medal at Athens. She conceded she was no expert, but in her view Eric should have been the Olympic champion. Eric answered her while never taking his eyes from mine. He acknowledged it was a disappointing outcome but he'd moved on from the experience by first moving to Australia, then returning to Germany after his circus adventure had run its course.

James introduced himself. I explained the coincidence and James offered Eric the chance to meet the cast at the end of the day.

"However, right now," he said, "we need to keep moving. You can reminisce later! It's a complicated sequence so let's catch up when we've wrapped. By the way, Mr Strom, would you be open to a speaking part? I need a Gypsy cook! It's not a glamorous role, but it would mean more money."

Eric nodded and thanked the young director. Tilda and I walked back to where the cameramen were preparing. Eric followed us. I asked him about Anthony, the other strongman from our circus days, and what happened to him.

"Anthony," Eric said, "is just over there."

Sure enough, Anthony was sitting on his haunches a short distance away looking at nothing in particular.

Notwithstanding my shock at running into my two former colleagues, I was able to pull myself together and concentrate. The scene was noisy and busy with a large crowd of Gypsies around us. There were two violinists playing traditional music which only added to the atmosphere. I became lost in character to the point where I completely forgot the cameramen and crew. The prodigal son's triumphant return to the family was a joyous occasion. He was my brother, and Henry's son, and we welcomed him back with open arms.

Kate Winslet's Viktoria was Daniel's wife. She adored him. Meanwhile, Eric had been instructed to cook whole fish over the open fire, calling out when one was ready to be eaten. The Gypsies ate them straight from the skewers and spat the bones on the ground. There was dancing, drinking, and raucous singing. The set up should have been logistically challenging (the cameramen were moving among us almost as if part of the troupe) and I wouldn't have been surprised if what ended up being a day's work had taken a week.

"You see," James explained, "in a way, this approach to filming, if executed correctly, can be easier because it's all one shot, or at least one shot from different cameras. For that reason, there being fewer interruptions and re-sets, the actors can, well, act in a way that would be nearly impossible if we were continually chopping and changing, re-applying makeup, and so on. It's a strange thing, but we will only use two or three minutes of this scene. Perhaps a few more. In a way, it would be fun to show the entire celebration of the glorious return of the Gaurige son as a complete sequence, but perhaps we should just use it in our *making of* documentary!"

Tilda invited me to the cabin. Before I opened the door I smelled pickled fish. I remembered Eric's fondness for seafood. He was sitting on the bed holding a bottle of home-made liquor in one hand and a jar of herrings in the other.

"Listen," Tilda said, "can you talk about the old days? Nick is so reluctant to reveal anything about his life and I know it must have been exciting."

✷

Eric and I had to be careful about what we revealed of *Circus Mundo.* We'd had our successes and friendships, but there were also dark times. He poured out four, not three, small glasses of the liquor. The reason became clear when there was a knock on the door. Tilda opened it and there was the giant figure of Anthony, Eric's partner of many years. He hadn't changed.

In no way were either of the strongmen intimidated by the presence of the world famous actor. They told as much as they could of our history together, glossing over the more unsavory details, including several fatal accidents. The show had been at crisis point, they said, both professionally and financially, until I'd taken over. There was no mention of the violence, jealousies, and fractured relationships that had ultimately destroyed our show. Instead, Eric and Anthony focused on the hard work involved in turning the operation from a small time traveling show into a performance-driven spectacle that had come close to establishing it as one of the best known variety shows on the east coast of Australia. It was a miracle I had reconnected with these larger than life characters after so much time. I felt both nostalgic and a little terrified.

Tilda proposed a toast to old friends as we downed our drinks. Unfortunately, the strong homemade liquor made her pass out immediately and fall backwards onto the bed. Tilda was mumbling to herself in what sounded like a foreign language. After being reassured by the German that she would recover by the morning, I asked Eric about the bronze medal he'd shown me many years ago—whether he'd finished in third place or, as Tilda had remembered, had not even managed a place on the dais.

"Tilda is technically correct," he said. "I finished just outside the medal places. However, the bronze medallist, Chechi, sent me his medal in recognition that, in his view, I should have won the gold. Chechi is a great champion and even greater human being. He knew, as we all did, Tampakos only took the gold because he was the local favorite."

At that moment, a bright flash lit up the front window of the cabin, half blinding me. The three of us ran outside to see a man with a camera run into the darkness.

The next day on all the internet news services there were stories about me and two unnamed performers from *The Secret* Writer in a room with an unconscious Tilda Swinton. Tilda didn't wake up until late and she couldn't remember any part of the previous evening apart from a moment of temporary blindness. She asked what in hell it was we'd been drinking, and I recounted how, in the circus days, Eric would make his own spirit from leftover food scraps. I told her I'd also experienced temporary blindness the first time I tasted it.

The photograph that accompanied the media blitz was blurry. Sandro Kopp's portrait of me, that Tilda had hung on the wall of the cabin, made it appear as if three men were looking at the famous and unconscious actress with sinister intentions. The moment was portrayed, and described as such in the accompanying articles, as a debaucherous night on the set of *The Secret Writer*. It was journalism at its worst but Tilda was philosophical.

"How many photographs have you seen," she asked, "of naked celebrities lying on their partners in a hotel room overlooking St Tropez? Often the cameramen, and they are nearly always men although an increasing number of young women are taking up the profession, will put their lives in danger to get one intimate shot, one that seeks to show our normality and how we are, in fact, just like everyone else. The idea is to display our imperfections, quite contrary to the way we come across in our public lives. It's a strange form of revenge. The extravagances and advantages of being a movie actor can only be experienced at a price which, of course, is our privacy and control over how we are portrayed—often in our most intimate moments. They build us up into deities and then take us down when we are at our most vulnerable. Also, Nick, don't forget it's a great story that someone can be plucked from the obscurity of the nine-to-five in a nowhere country and be paid hundreds of thousands of pounds to be a film actor. But it's a double-edged sword, my darling. It suggests there is an opportunity out there for everyone to make a move like yours. However, on the other hand, there will also be a high degree of jealousy, not just from the everyday person who takes an interest in the lives of the famous, but from hardworking actors who will go their entire lives without getting the break you or I, or the rest of us, have been fortunate enough to have been offered. I'm not *blaming* you, Nick, I'm just trying to provide an explanation."

We arrived on set a little later than the others. Daniel, Alan, James, and Kate gathered around Tilda and me. I detected a world-weariness in Alan, or perhaps it was some sort of profound regret, before he shook it off by calling us together to hear from James who had either ignored or was impervious to the most recent scandal.

"Good morning! And let's put the latest piece of unfortunate news to one side and just concentrate. Today's shoot, as you know, is focused on Viktoria Asarov. We'll be bringing into much sharper focus her dual roles as the great but unknown Russian novelist and key part of the Gypsy narrative. It's crucial we don't restrict her character, or let her be pulled into the Gaurige plotline, without reminding the audience she is everywhere. Viktoria in London will become, or already is, part of the Gaurige family. She is telling her own Gypsy history. At the same time, while being central to the Sachsenwald action, she will simultaneously be writing the novel the audience is experiencing. It will be my job to ensure this is clearly drawn out but, and I was talking to Alan and Kate about this last night, we will need to add a deeper level of subtlety to our performances to make this happen. The relationships between you all will have to be close, while at the same time maintaining a certain distance from Viktoria. Do you all understand?"

I appreciated what James was aiming for. His instructions reminded me of my first reading of the screenplay and our initial discussions about the project. Viktoria had to be a key part of the action but at the same time above it, because she was writing the story as it was happening. If James could manage it, it would result in something that hadn't been achieved before.

"Nick," James instructed, "it's your turn to take Viktoria under your wing as she, or should I say Maria Gaurige, finds love and acceptance for the first time. It is the appreciation and respect she has been looking for all her life but *please and another please,* remember she is a part of you and the family, but simultaneously exists outside it, entering the action only to inform her novel and write the profound sadness that underpins it."

I needed to find another gear with my performance. So far, although I wouldn't say it had been easy, I'd been able to slot in without too much trouble. James and the director of photography had pulled me up a few times, but it was mostly reminding me where the camera was. They taught me how I needed to both consider and ignore it. There were some issues with my accent but they were quickly rectified with the help of the voice coach. I realized now that the subtlety and complex duality being asked of Kate's Viktoria/Maria applied to each of us. After all, Viktoria was a Gaurige, but so was Karl Marx, Friedrich Engels, and Jenny von Westphalen.

Behind James I noticed Eric and Anthony scratching at the dirt with large sticks. They were trying to get my attention but I didn't have time to talk to them before shooting started.

The scenes I found most difficult were the intimate ones with Viktoria, who had surely written the novel, at least in part, to give her life a semblance of love. Thankfully, Kate was sensitive to my unease at being physically affectionate in front of the camera with a relative stranger. As requested by James, Daniel and Tilda maintained a distant, almost dream-like presence. On one level they needn't have been in the scene at all but on another it was crucial in rendering Viktoria's imagination. Daniel selflessly disappeared into the periphery.

Alan Rickman's Henry Gaurige was a revelation. It was he who was the counterpoint to Kate's Viktoria. While her performance had to be so carefully calibrated, jumping between worlds, Alan allowed the rest of us to work around him and reveal the deepest parts of Viktoria's vision.

When James called an end to proceedings after a few hours,

I thought it would be to ask us to do the scene again. However, he clapped his hands with a loud *cut!* We would break so he could do a rough edit of the days' filming and play it back to us in the afternoon. Things were progressing well, and I think it was because of the organic approach. The location, the multi-textured narrative, and the acting challenges were supposed to test us, but perhaps these difficulties brought us together.

Eric and Anthony approached me. They'd found the paparazzo who had taken the photograph the previous evening. I was surprised that whoever had taken the shot would have remained in the forest overnight. It was relatively mild during the day, but overnight the temperature dropped to just one or two degrees.

Having overheard the conversation and no doubt interested in meeting the mystery cameraman, Tilda followed us. Some two hundred meters from where we'd been filming, Eric pointed to a man who was lying on the ground. His neck was broken, the head at a right-angle from the shoulders. It was the chauffeur who'd betrayed us at Pinewood. The man whose father had co-written *Invisible*. A professional *Ricoh* camera with a telephoto lens was hanging on its strap from one of the branches of the Elm tree that towered over the body. Tilda suggested he must have been hiding in the branches and fallen to his death.

"Certainly," she said, pointing to the camera, "if he fell from that height it would be enough to kill him. They will do anything to get their photo and, on this occasion, he was unlucky—but not before he'd sent it to every tabloid in the world."

Anthony, who'd said little since we reconnected, recommended we call the authorities immediately to ensure the matter could be dealt with as soon as possible. An episode like this could derail the film for weeks. We all agreed and summoned James and Alan. Daniel and Kate, who had no doubt heard the commotion, weren't far behind. Daniel asked for a phone and, having touched the paparazzo's neck with this finger, called the authorities to report, in German, there had been a fatality on set. *Ein Mann ist tod.* I asked Eric whether there could be another explanation for the accident. He quickly assured us the facts were quite clear.

"It appears," he said, "the cameraman was hiding in the tree after Anthony and I chased him last night. The forest was so dark we lost him almost immediately. He was too quick on his feet."

Anthony reached up with his stick and hooked the camera down from the branch. He pointed out some of the technical features, including the in-built email functionality and optical zoom, and then pushed a button to view the photographs. We huddled around the surprisingly large screen. There were a number that looked like test shots, but then we came upon hundreds of photos he'd taken of us in the forest. Many were of the cast and crew preparing for the day ahead. There was an intimate shot of Tilda and me, deep in conversation, and a lovely and revealing photo of Kate and James with his left hand on her cheek. Daniel was in the background with a pipe in his mouth, smoke rising from it. Despite the gravity of the situation, I couldn't help but appreciate the photographs as very beautiful. They were candid, but looked staged.

Tilda commented that the dead man had quite an eye and even suggested some of the photographs could be used for promotional purposes. I was inclined to agree. The shots captured the essence of actors at work. Kate said if the circumstances were different and if he'd only approached James with his ideas, he could have worked with us to capture the process. I told the team about my experience of the return trip from Scotland and the visit to Carlisle. Alan said the photographer must have come from a talented family. *Invisible* had been one of his favorite songs of the 1980s and certainly the Moyet track he liked the most.

The Hamburg police arrived and questioned each of us about our relationship with the poor fellow. *The Secret Writer* was delayed while the cause of death was confirmed.

Claire, who had been largely absent from the shoot (she'd gone to Los Angeles with Elliot) turned up on resumption of filming. They'd decided Tilda and I needed security to ensure we could work without distractions. Eric and Anthony would be our bodyguards for the duration of the production. From that point on we never had cause to feel in any danger.

"Perhaps," Daniel joked, "your two friends are proactively taking out all unsavory types before they get within range!"

It was hard to believe we'd arrived so quickly at the last day of filming in the Sachsenwald. The most dramatic part of the story was about to be played out. The scene focused on Viktoria as Henrietta Gaurige, the eldest and most beautiful of Henry's daughters, and Daniel, this time playing Markus, a Gypsy from another clan. They had been matched by the two families. They would marry, irrespective of their wishes. Henrietta and Markus were meeting for the first time, neither convinced of the arrangement. Initially circumspect about spending the rest of their lives with a complete stranger, Markus and Henrietta fall instantly in love. It was surely symbolic of Viktoria's need for love and acceptance, this time with the real figure of her desire—Karl Marx/Markus the Gypsy.

After their meeting, it being clear to both families there should be no delay to the union, there was a wedding celebration that mirrored the intensity of that for Henry's son after his family's return. There was a fire, and Eric was again called upon to act as cook. The rest of the cast, including extras, moved across the set in a state of great animation, the cameramen moving in and around us.

After the dialogue had finished, James let the scene carry on until the party came to a natural conclusion. As shooting continued the fire burnt down to its embers and Eric served the last of the fish to the revelers. I noticed Daniel sneak away to his caravan. He returned with a violin. I wondered if he'd made it himself. Daniel started dancing and playing Gypsy folk music at the same time. His fingers moved at lightning speed and a group of us, Kate, Tilda, Alan, some of the extras, and me, joined hands and danced around him in a circle. When one of us became too tired we would split from the group, whereupon Eric or Anthony would thrust a tiny glass of home-made liquor into our hands.

James, surely sensing a moment of cinematic history in the making, kept the cameras rolling. As a result, he filmed a performance that, in the end, had little to do with a movie production. Rather, it captured a collective desire to give Viktoria the love and respect she deserved. There were so many threads of the story being brought together. I felt them running through my veins.

The cameramen stopped filming and they too joined the festivities. James walked into what had been a film set but was now a celebration of the end of our adventure in the

Sachsenwald. Eric's liquor was being passed around. We were a happy band of Gypsies drinking straight from the bottle. Even Daniel lost his legendary self control. At one point he was plucking his violin with one hand while drinking from the other. I wondered if he'd learned the violin especially for the movie or been taught as a child.

There were hundreds of us losing all inhibition and without any thought for what an outside observer might think. One sip of Eric's drink was enough to make you lose your mind, but we drank it like water. Claire and James had reconnected and were kissing passionately against a giant spruce. Many of the extras, those not dancing around the fire and throwing pieces of clothing into the air, were touching each other intimately. Daniel was leaning into Kate so closely their lips were almost touching.

As evening fell, the group slowly returned to its senses. Daniel made his way to his caravan and the extras walked slowly to the bus that would take them back to their hotel. After the noise and debauchery, a silence fell over the forest. Tilda, Eric, Anthony, and I were the only ones remaining. Eric picked up the empty bottles, four in each hand, presumably so he could re-use them for another batch. I felt an incredible fatigue as if all the thinking, effort, and considerable change I'd experienced had only at that moment landed on my shoulders.

Tilda asked me, recalling nothing of the previous two hours, what had happened. I wasn't sure what to say. It was hard to know if our experiences were real or the alcohol-induced imaginings of people desperate for release from overwhelming, creative pressures. It was an exhilarating feeling to know *The Secret Writer* was close to realization, but at the same time there were parts of my former life I missed—routine things like printing and binding business reports. There is something delicious about meaningless activity that fills time.

The next day we made our way to Hamburg International Airport. Not for the first time, I felt a strong desire to return to Sydney.

On our arrival in England I wondered whether we could maintain our energy levels. It felt like we were starting all over again as we drove north to Pinewood to do incidentals and re-shoots—and of course start the complex editing process. The team would also be preparing for Kate's St Petersburg scenes. James' enthusiasm was undaunted, however, as he spoke about the challenges of editing the Sachsenwald sequences.

"I want to use as much footage as possible," he said, "but am not yet sure how to *intersperse* the many hours of filming into meaningful Asarov vignettes."

On reviewing the earlier footage in the studio, I expressed my concern about Engels and whether my performance had enough emotional range.

"Nick," James reassured me, "don't underestimate your Friedrich. You are a figure of reliability and strength and, in a way, the anchor for the action around him. Engels is the wise counsel. Without you, Viktoria would never have been employed. You also reassure Jenny about Viktoria's presence in the household. Remember how you tell her she has nothing to worry about regarding any emotional attachment? This leads inexorably to the attachment between you and Jenny in the Sachsenwald. Asarov the prescient writer has sensed the feelings you have for each other and played them out in her novel. Do you see how, without Engels, the story would lack that stable influence but Deleuzian spark? The other thing I would point out is that I don't believe any other actor in the world would have, or could have, built the character and engaged with the other actors with the same degree of *under-performance*. I really must make a point of thanking Elliot for finding you, although of course you were there all along."

Anthony, who was by now ever present with his partner Eric, laughed and said I was not only a fine circus administrator but a good enough performer as well.

A little later, back in England, I heard Claire and Elliot discussing whether the St Petersburg scenes, in which we first get to know Viktoria Asarov and understand her motivations, should be shot on location or at Pinewood. Having seen the results of the ultra-realistic and improvisational approach in the Sachsenwald, the producer wanted to make sure the balance of the film was equally authentic and had asked for a cost-benefit analysis of the two options. Eventually, despite being significantly more expensive, Elliot waved away any concerns and opted for the production to move to Russia. James was excited at the prospect of filming where many of his cinematic and literary heroes had been born.

"Imagine," he said, "we will be treading in the footsteps of Tarkovsky, Tolstoy, Eldar Ryazanov, Todorovsky. Perhaps we could meet Yuri Kara!"

James' enthusiasm was infectious. I wished him well, knowing I wouldn't be required. Because I had no further part to play, I could either stay in England or return to Sydney until the production was complete. Finally, I'd have time to turn my attention to the many emails and text messages the Executive Director had sent me. I felt a little guilty about not being as contactable or communicative as I could have been. Perhaps it meant the change process was going well and with full staff buy-in.

However, to my surprise (and Tilda was also a little taken aback) James invited us to join them in Russia for what would surely be a new adventure.

"Why not?" he asked. "The team isn't complete without you."

Two days later we were at Heathrow airport boarding a Lufthansa flight direct to St Petersburg. The entire business and first class sections had been reserved. The giant frames of Eric and Anthony were sitting behind Tilda and me. I hadn't expected them to be coming, but Elliot had insisted they provide ongoing security given they had so far done such an excellent job. It was true that since they'd come on board, notwithstanding the unfortunate death of the photographer, there had been no incidents.

Daniel was staying in England. He was putting the finishing touches to his medieval Irish sailing boat. He now wanted to sail across the Atlantic for the Academy Awards presentation, rather than the shorter voyage across the Irish Sea.

On the flight from London to St Petersburg I was surprised to see the in-flight entertainment carried a retrospective of Daniel Day Lewis' films. Tilda fell asleep as soon as the plane rose into the air. Eric and Anthony were playing a card game I recognized from the circus days. They'd tried to explain the rules many years ago but it was one of those games where the rules change depending on the suit. Hearts were most valuable, then diamonds, clubs, and spades. Anthony said it was like Bolivia but with only one deck of cards. Eric compared it to Gin Rummy but the one time I played with them they laughed loudly whenever I put a card down. They told me I was lucky we weren't playing for money. There was no clear logic and I quickly gave up, much to their amusement.

I started watching *In the Name of the Father.*

It was strange to see Daniel in a movie after having to come to know him as a fellow professional. The film was about the Guildford Four—three Irishmen and one Irish woman who were wrongly convicted for an IRA bombing in the 1970s. The English police, desperate for a conviction to appease the public and their political masters, fabricated evidence and concealed information that would have ensured they were never sent to prison. Confessions were forced out of the four through brutal and illegal interrogation methods. Daniel played Gerry Connolly who was sent to prison with his father. Connolly wrote a book about the horrors of the experience.

It was a tragic story, to say the least, and by the end of the movie I was close to tears. While the plot was straightforward from a narrative perspective, the characterizations of these real-life people were extraordinary. But, for me, it was Daniel who stood out above the rest. From the first moment I encountered Gerry Connolly I forgot the actor completely. Given the duration of the journey, I only saw fifteen minutes of *My Left Foot,* in which Daniel played Christy Brown, a man who suffered from cerebral palsy.

Tilda slept through the entire flight. Eric and Anthony were still playing cards when they were instructed to fold away their tray tables for landing.

✴

Tilda and I spent the first morning on set with Kate Winslet and a very fine local actress who played the role of Viktoria's colleague at the library through whom she became acquainted with the work of Karl Marx. We then decided to spend a few days walking the streets of St. Petersburg.

Despite our protestations, James insisted, on Elliot's advice, that Eric and Anthony accompany us. They were discreet and kept their distance. We often didn't know they were there, or thought we had managed to lose them, but they appeared from nowhere whenever anyone approached us. Tilda was well known in Russia. She was asked for her autograph on a number of occasions, and to my surprise a young man asked for mine. I was touched by this even though it was unclear whether he knew anything about me or had asked only because I was with the world-famous actress.

Those who approached were respectful of Tilda and delighted when she took a moment to sign her name and inquire which of her movies the autograph seeker liked the most. The young fellow who had so politely asked for my signature said his favorite was *Michael Clayton*. This pleased Tilda very much. She said to me later her co-star in that film, George Clooney, was a much underrated actor, perhaps because his political beliefs put him too far to the liberal side of the Hollywood aristocracy. Tilda thought he should stretch himself by taking on films with foreign directors and working in another language.

She suggested we take a St Petersburg street car so we could have a proper look at the city and suburbs. It was a good idea. The tram took us past important cultural sites like the

Hermitage Museum and St Isaac's Cathedral, but we also visited anonymous suburban streets which gave us a real taste of the city and how its people lived. We stopped in small coffee houses and enjoyed pirozhky and oladi.

On the tram ride back to our hotel I noticed the young man who had asked for our autographs some hours earlier, the *Michael Clayton* fan, was sitting a few seats away. He walked past Eric and Anthony (the latter stood up to follow him), sat opposite us, and described, in imperfect but easily understandable English, how it was his dream to become a professional actor. He'd acted in local theatre productions but the state of the Russian film industry was not as robust as that of England or America. He was finding it hard to break through. No doubt feeling some pressure as a result of his manner, Tilda wanted nothing further to do with him. However, when we got off the tram, a short distance from the hotel, he started walking alongside us, persistently asking for help in finding work in Hollywood. He didn't seem aggressive but was certainly a little unhinged.

Unfortunately, just as we were approaching the busy Nevsky Prospekt, the young man jumped out in front of oncoming traffic and was terribly injured. I immediately went to his aid. The driver of the car that hit the young actor called for an ambulance, which arrived after a few minutes. It appeared that one of the man's legs was broken, and he was visibly distressed as he was carefully placed in the back of the vehicle. Two police cars arrived as it drove off with its siren blaring.

Eric and Anthony had disappeared. Tilda and I were taken to the central police station where we made statements. Both our accounts were to the effect that the fellow had been following us back to our hotel, wanting us to help him get work in the film industry. He had become increasingly obstinate.

The policemen and women, who were all largely uninterested in the accident, were delighted to have a movie star at the station. Before we knew it, a group of ten or so officers emerged and crowded around us. A middle-aged woman in uniform laughed as she repeated the word *Narnia*, excited to inform Tilda she had seen *The Lion, the Witch and the Wardrobe* with her children. It was a strangely charming situation. We accepted a glass of vodka from a senior police officer.

Unlike other mishaps that had befallen us, there was no accompanying media circus. The incident passed unnoticed and we returned to the studio to find Kate and James finishing their day's work. The set was styled as a library filled with dusty books in no apparent order. They were all bound in leather and if not printed in the middle of the nineteenth century, they certainly looked like they had been. I picked one up and although it was printed in the Russian alphabet I recognized Dostoyevsky's name. James took the book from me.

"The first time I read *The Idiot*," he said as he turned the book over in his hands, "I was fifteen years old. I read it because I'd spent every Sunday evening for two months watching the BBC serialization. After I finished the book I immediately saw the faults with the English version—short cuts with plot and characterization—even the atmosphere was misplaced. They made the mood so dreary when it's a novel of rich promise. Of course, by that stage of my life I already had an idea I'd make movies, but after I read Dostoyevsky, I *knew* I would. For that reason, this book will always be an inspiration to me. Perhaps we could do our own version!"

At that moment, two policemen walked into the studio. The larger of the two introduced himself. He explained, in excellent English albeit with a heavy accent, that the man injured earlier in the afternoon had accused one of our bodyguards of throwing him into oncoming traffic.

Obviously, this was a concern for everyone. On the face of it, without testing the accusations, it seemed Eric and Anthony may have taken their responsibilities too seriously. The senior officer, a Detective Inspector no less, informed us that the young man's statement was of the most serious nature, and none of us should take the matter lightly.

"In some circles," he said, "it is acceptable for the rich and famous to get away with murder, but I am not that sort of policeman."

I was surprised at his expert English. I thought about complimenting him but thought better of it. The Inspector reached into his briefcase from which he extracted a laptop computer. He asked if we had a projection device. Claire, who had been listening carefully to the Russian, took the laptop and plugged it into a monitor. The Inspector showed us grainy CCTV video of the minutes leading up to the moment the young man was injured. Although the quality of the video was poor, you could make out Tilda and I about to cross Nevsky Prospekt, standing at the lights, and waiting for the signal. We had our heads turned in the direction of the luckless actor, away from the eye of the camera, listening to his clumsy and increasingly aggressive requests for assistance with his career. Eric and Anthony had placed themselves between us and him as a protective measure. Anthony turned side on, talking to us and apparently looking directly up at the CCTV camera. He brought his giant frame so close he blocked any view of Eric and the young man. I remembered the moment. In the next frame the young Russian actor flew through the air and was hit by a car traveling at high speed.

"As you can see," said the Inspector, "the actions of these two men have led to serious injuries—injuries from which it is unlikely there will be a full recovery. I can assure you I will not let this matter rest until I understand exactly what happened. I ask you to inform me where they are so I can interview them personally."

It was a strong warning from a man used to wielding significant power.

✶

To my mind, although the CCTV footage *looked* damning, it was inconclusive. The most worrying aspect was Anthony's apparent awareness of the camera, which was placed high up on a building just across the intersection. If the two strongmen had done anything wrong, without having read the statement of the victim, the only thing pointing to a crime was when the Inspector froze the footage at the precise moment Anthony, allegedly, obscured the actions of his partner.

"Images can be deceiving," James said. "It looks to me as if Anthony is just doing his job and protecting his clients from the unwanted attention of a dangerous fan."

The Inspector disagreed. He had interviewed the young man and there was no doubt in his mind. He wasn't intending to let an international film production get in the way of his investigation. Again, I was struck by the Inspector's impeccable English. He must have studied or spent time in America or England. His expression was faultless and, unlike many people speaking English as a second language, he never omitted the definite or indefinite article.

Tilda outlined how the victim, although initially polite, had become increasingly desperate.

"He approached us looking for an opportunity," she offered, "confident we would be able to meet his request for work in the industry. But his efforts became more insistent as we approached the hotel, presumably because he knew as soon as we were inside he would lose contact with us. I would be surprised if the allegations are not an attempt at blackmail."

The inspector dismissed this hypothesis and asked for the names of the strongmen and their whereabouts. He wanted to interview them and gauge their reactions to the CCTV footage. I gave him the names Eric Strom and Anthony. I had no idea of Anthony's surname. It had never occurred to me to ask and in all my dealings with him it had never been necessary to know.

The Inspector was incredulous.

"*Eric Strom*, do you mean the German gymnast? The same Eric Strom who was denied the gold medal at the Athens Olympics? My son competed against him in the still rings but he could only manage eighth. It was a strong field, but Strom should have won. The judging on that day remains a blight on the sport. I need to speak to him."

Although the coincidence was incredible, I couldn't help but think *blight* was an interesting word for a foreign speaker to choose.

Needless to say, we were all amazed the Inspector knew Eric. The way he described what happened in the final of the still rings event at Athens was entirely consistent with Tilda's recollection. The Russian provided further insight into Strom's career.

"You see Strom was," the Inspector revealed, "at least six inches taller than any other competitor. To some, including a number of judges, this either gave him a slightly ungainly appearance when performing or, and this was surely the most unfair aspect of it all, his height gave him some sort of advantage over other competitors. Perhaps it was for these reasons he was only able to win medals at events less prestigious than the Olympics. There is a story that Chechi gave his bronze medal to Strom in recognition he should at least have been on the dais. I know, having spoken to Chechi at length about the matter, he thought Strom the best gymnast of his generation."

The Inspector, having only minutes before indicated his intention to ensure justice for the victim, even if that meant charging Eric and Anthony with attempted murder, now expressed the deepest sympathy for the gymnast.

"In many countries," he went on, "your sexuality is not a big deal. But in Russia you can be thrown into prison for the slightest indiscretion. Think of that what you want. I couldn't care less what people do with their personal lives. However, the International Gymnastics Federation, over which some very socially conservative countries have a strong influence, has a very dim view of such things. In my opinion, Strom's career was derailed by factors that should have nothing to do with sport. He was a supremely gifted athlete but he had to deal with the destabilizing influence of his father. The father's life would be defined only by the success of the son. After the debacle at Athens, I don't believe they ever spoke to each other again. It was a tragedy. My own son Yuri, although an elite athlete like Strom…well I appreciated his dedication no matter whether he won or lost. I watched his career from when he was unbeatable at school and district level all the way to when he was found wanting against only the very best in the world. I couldn't be prouder of him."

The Inspector had tears in his eyes as he described his love for Yuri.

"The last thing I knew," the Inspector concluded, "Strom had disappeared. No-one knew what happened to him. It was a terrible shame because he gave so much to the sport. So many athletes are left broken. I would very much like to see him again."

I sensed Tilda wanted to say something about Eric and Australia, but I touched her arm to let her know it was not the time for such things. I thought it best to allow Eric to tell his own story, if indeed he wanted to.

Claire, who like the rest of us had been silent up to that point, decided to take action. She suggested we go to the hotel to find Eric and Anthony. The Inspector and his colleague, who had remained silent during this initial stage of the investigation, led us outside to a police van in which there was more than enough room for me, Tilda, Kate, James, and

Claire. The two rear seats were arranged so I was facing the front and looking directly at the Inspector. The junior officer was driving.

In the drama of the preceding half hour I hadn't noticed a scar that stretched from the bottom of the Inspector's chin to the top of his shirt button. It may have reached further. I'd also failed to take in the breadth of his shoulders. He was a little overweight, like many police officers, but his physical presence was imposing, not unlike that of the two men he would shortly be interviewing. The journey to the hotel passed without a word. The driver turned on the flashing light and we sped through the streets, vehicles moving out of the way to allow us through.

The Inspector asked the concierge for Eric and Anthony's room pass. Having reached the twenty-first floor where the two men were staying, he placed the card over the electronic lock. The junior officer pulled a pistol and held it at his side. The Inspector told him off in Russian and the gun was placed back in its holster. Upon entering the suite we found Eric and Anthony sitting either side of a large coffee table. They were playing cards and drinking tiny bottles of mini-bar spirits. The bottles looked ridiculous in their giant hands. They looked unsurprised by our visit and who was visiting them. Eric stood up.

"Yuri Bulgarov," Eric said, as if expecting the encounter, "it must be fifteen years since I last saw you. How is your son? I haven't heard from him in a long time, but then I have lost touch with so many people since I left the world of gymnastics. It feels like it was someone else's life."

The Inspector composed himself as he looked Eric up and down, as if having to convince himself this was indeed the great gymnast.

"You have hardly changed, Eric. I will never forget the help you gave Yuri junior. He had a genuine love for the sport but never the talent, or the will, to dominate. Perhaps the latter is more important to achieve at the highest level. That's what made Chechi great, and even you if I may say."

"That's all in the past," Eric said. "Don't worry about me, my life has been very fulfilling since the Olympics. I worked in Australia as a performance artist, met my dear friend Anthony whose life has in many ways been similar to mine, and now I have acted in a movie. These have all been quite unexpected and happy developments."

"There will be plenty of time for reminiscing," the Inspector answered, "but for the moment I need to ask about an actor who will be in hospital for some months at least. He has two broken legs and his pelvis is in pieces. He may never walk again."

James and Claire were staring at Eric and Anthony. Tilda was holding my hand. I'd almost forgotten Kate who was looking through the window at the street below. She hadn't had time to change out of her costume and was still wearing a full-length dress in a muted floral pattern. Her hair was done up in the tidy Victorian style.

Although I'd expected Eric to lead the conversation with the Inspector, given they knew each other, it was Anthony who spoke first. Rather than responding to the question of how the young man came to be so terribly injured, he instead asked the Inspector how he'd happened to get the scar on his neck. The Inspector was surprised at the question, as might be expected in the circumstances, but said many people asked him about it.

"I am from a sporting family. My brothers were excellent gymnasts, although not to Eric's level. I, on the other hand, was a speed skater, because I wanted to follow in my mother's footsteps—those of the great Tatiana Likhareva. I don't believe in false modesty so I will say I was very good. Just as good as my mother, if not better. I was cut down by an arch rival while training for the 1972 Sapporo Winter Olympics. I will not do him the honour of mentioning his name. My competitor, who I admit was fast and perhaps my equal, sliced down my neck with one of his skates. Anyone watching may have thought it was an accident, but I knew otherwise. The matter never went to court. He was protected by the authorities and the regime was in no mood for scandals. By the time I recovered, my best years were behind me. The criminal didn't even win a medal. I entered the police force and can't complain. I have a good life and am well-respected. However, like Mr Strom, I don't want to get caught up in the past and become nostalgic. I am here for quite different reasons. I would like you to explain what happened on the Nevsky Prospekt."

Anthony took the floor.

"The young fellow," he said, "was disturbed and unstable. There was no doubt in my mind there was a serious risk to Tilda Swinton and Nick Clement. We placed ourselves between our clients and the young man, who then threatened us, calling us all sorts of things I couldn't understand. I think he had a knife. We were shocked when he jumped in front of the traffic, but just before he did so he said, in English, if he couldn't be an actor his life was worth nothing. Eric and I...well there was, I admit, an element of panic in leaving the scene so quickly. I apologize for our actions in that respect. It is unforgivable but I doubt it's a crime. However, being otherwise entirely blameless and in a foreign city, I think it's understandable."

Anthony's explanation came across as reasonable, and there was no evidence, other than the word of the young actor, to suggest anything untoward had happened.

"Unfortunately," said Inspector Bulgarov, "your account is totally at odds with the complainant's. It could not be more different."

In response to Eric's questions about whether there was any physical evidence linking him and Anthony to the incident, the Inspector admitted there was none. Anthony asked whether there was anything at all apart from the man's statement.

"All I have," Bulgarov answered, "is his account and the CCTV footage. I will show it to you now."

He extracted his laptop and played the video again.

"Why did you, Anthony, choose that precise moment to block the camera's view of your partner? You are looking at the camera as if you knew it was there."

"As it turns out," Anthony replied, "I did see the camera. Having spent my formative years in the boxing ring I am always on the lookout for the unexpected and can't deny it came into my line of vision. I distinctly remember the moment. The truth is I was doing my job, protecting Nick and Tilda in an unpredictable situation. You can't lock me up for noticing a camera!"

I had no reason to doubt Anthony's story. Although the incident was shocking at the time, neither Tilda nor I had witnessed anything that would suggest attempted murder. I said as much to the Inspector, to which he replied, quite rightly, that I couldn't possibly have seen anything given Anthony was blocking my view.

On the laptop screen the young man's brief flight through the air was frozen before rolling on in slow motion. But it revealed nothing. From one frame to the next all you could see was Anthony turning side-on, his eye looking over our heads to the camera, then the flight into the path of the car. Of course it was a terrible thing to see, made no less so seeing it a second time, but I couldn't believe, even knowing what Eric and Anthony were capable of, they would do anything so foolish in public. The Inspector stood up. He would take formal statements from both sides and be in touch about the next steps. He looked at Eric.

"I always admired you," Bulgarov said. "There were many obstacles placed in your path and you overcame them. Even though the number one ranking was never yours, the gymnastics community knew better. Do you, my son, and Chechi still write to each other? Even though Yuri is now a tradesman and Chechi is in sports administration, they find the time to stay in touch. Perhaps when this has all passed, irrespective of the outcome, we can sit down and talk. I would like to know what happened to you after you left Germany."

Eric commented that these were not the ideal circumstances for a reunion but he nevertheless thanked the Inspector for his interest. As the policemen were leaving the hotel room the younger officer received a phone call. The conversation ended and he whispered to his superior. The Inspector announced that the young actor had died of his injuries. Eric and Anthony returned to their card game.

We stayed another week in St Petersburg, which was enough time for Kate to complete her work. Tilda and I weren't in the mood for more sightseeing. We stayed in the hotel or went with Eric and Anthony to the studio.

Kate's work was effortless. She turned Viktoria Asarov from a nervous young woman lacking in confidence to one who was prepared (remarkably given what it must have been like to have been an artistic woman in the nineteenth century) to take risks of the greatest proportions. The texture of her acting was so precisely measured you could barely notice the gradual psychological transition. For the last time, James called *cut*. As he finished reviewing the day's footage, he said he had all he needed to make a great movie.

The atmosphere was sombre. Daniel was absent and there had been the controversy with Eric and Anthony, but I don't believe those were the reasons for the downbeat mood. The last months had been full of so much hard work, and James was overwhelmed. The young director, plucked from obscurity and surrounded by the world's greatest actors, was suddenly struck by the enormity of it all. Kate went to him, held his hands in hers and reminded him the work wasn't over yet. There was the small matter of post-production and making the film ready for the screen. James held her to him, tears streaming down his cheeks and said *thank you everyone*, over and over again.

"Nick, thank you for reading the script and giving me the confidence I needed. Claire, I know things have been difficult for us, but thank you for believing in me. Tilda, I have admired your work for so long and it has been a privilege to work with you. Elliot! Where is Elliot?"

Claire reminded him Elliot had returned to Los Angeles, negotiating film rights for a novel by Jay McInerney. James' phone rang. It was Daniel Day Lewis, who asked to be put on speaker.

"Congratulations to you all," he said, his voice delayed by

a second or two. "I believe the world is ready for *The Secret Writer*. It's been an experience of new experiences. However, with great achievement and success can come great sadness. I regret that it's my task to inform you that Alan Rickman passed away this morning."

I didn't know Alan well but had spent enough time with him to appreciate his genius. Not only was he an actor of great distinction who was able to take lead and supporting roles, but I'd witnessed first hand his enthusiasm for his craft, his ability to draw people together to test new ideas, and work through challenges. A deep sadness fell over us. We held each other before Claire suggested we return to the hotel and have a valedictory dinner.

At the restaurant, no-one, with the exception of Eric and Anthony, ate anything. We sat in silence and drank heavily, returning to our rooms with heavy hearts. Tilda and I were awake for the rest of the night. No doubt trying to take her mind away from the harrowing last few days, she mused on my life.

"You've had an interesting life," she said. "A country upbringing, a circus administrator, a role in business, and now an acting career. And whatever happened to the work you and Claire were doing on the organizational redesign? It seemed to be going somewhere. Do you think it's time to pick up the pieces? In the context of everything we've experienced it might be a welcome distraction to concentrate on something else entirely. I always feel a terrible emptiness after the shoot is over."

I appreciated Tilda's insight. We needed a distraction. I picked up my phone and checked my emails. There were, as usual, a number of messages from the Executive Director. Most were asking where I was and reminding me to keep in touch. One said I shouldn't hesitate to *reach out* if I needed anything. The most recent email had an attachment. The document was titled *Creating a New Organization – A Future Plan for Engagement*.

My advice was being sought on yet another, longer term plan for working in a completely different way. There were recommendations I was already familiar with, but the latest version went further than I'd ever imagined. It not only included employee engagement and feedback mechanisms, which were becoming more standard in the modern business world, but there were detailed floor plans with more break out and meeting rooms than actual desk space. There was a strong focus on mobility and teamwork. There would be technology enhancements to make it possible to collaborate from anywhere.

That night I, with Tilda's help, wrote a detailed reply to my

Executive Director, acknowledging the excellent approach to employee engagement and productivity. The break out rooms would have coffee machines and day beds. Breakfast, lunch, and dinner would be provided in common eating areas to encourage staff to meet people they may not otherwise work with. If you needed to meet an urgent deadline, you could work through the night and make use of the bathroom and sleeping facilities. The plan would completely reinvent the way we think about work.

I remarked to Tilda that the initial work Claire and I had done, which we thought progressive for a conservative firm, was merely a precursor to a much grander and more radical project. Tilda, in our defence, pointed out our initial assignment had been cast in relatively modest terms, and it was hardly in our remit to suggest such significant changes.

"Ultimately," she went on, "your work was the catalyst for action. You both did what you thought was right. But remember, radical change if not thoughtfully implemented can become unstuck. The company will need to take a gradual approach to implementation or you will lose staff and corporate knowledge. It's not enough to have a plan—you have to carry it out. Look at James as an example of how to project manage and deliver at the same time."

Tilda's views were interesting. Claire and I had discussed how many people, used to working in a particular way, may not want to make adjustments and may leave the company, possibly taking clients with them. As I sent my reply to the

Executive Director, Tilda sat up in bed and stared into space. I, too, was suddenly overcome with emotion.

In the arrivals area at Heathrow there were box sets of Rickman's movies for sale. It seemed inconceivable a product like that could be pulled together so quickly and Claire, like all of us, was disappointed by the flagrant commercialization. There were five DVDs in the set: *Truly, Madly, Deeply*; *Galaxy Quest*; *Sense and Sensibility*; *Die Hard*; and *Harry Potter and the Sorcerer's Stone*.

"Isn't it enough that we have lost such a great man? Can't the industry let him rest in peace? Don't get me wrong, a retrospective of his work is a great idea but surely they could have waited a few months, if only to *pretend* it wasn't just a money making exercise."

"It's a hastily compiled collection," James commented, "but nonetheless each of the performances is quite brilliant. It's strange...in much of his work Alan comes across as gruff or downright evil, but there is a hidden depth to him. There is always something behind his characterizations he won't reveal. It's what we don't see that is most telling. It is now my mission to make *The Secret Writer* the film Alan would have been proud of. Everything I do from this point on will be an *homage* to him."

As we drove off, I saw Sandro Kopp on the footpath. He'd

obviously been waiting for Tilda but somehow had missed both our arrival and departure.

After we arrived in Islington from Heathrow, Tilda half-heartedly suggested we spend some time in Scotland. I declined the offer. It was becoming apparent our relationship had been fuelled by the excitement of working together and was now in decline. Tilda didn't press the matter. James and Claire were returning to Pinewood, and while wondering whether I would go with them or return to Australia, James said he would like my assistance editing *The Secret Writer*.

"We are," he said, "on a strict timetable to get the movie ready and in cinemas in time for the awards season. There's even a financial bonus if the film gets so much as a nomination! Not that any of that really matters but if we can get a modicum of success for this film, hopefully it will enable me to make another. I have some ideas but suffice to say I would like to explore the trajectory your life has taken! *Circus Mundo* for god's sake!"

The next day Claire, Eric, Anthony, Kate, James, and I traveled by helicopter to Pinewood.

James, Claire, and I went to the editing suite first thing in the morning. Eric and Anthony came to the studio but the Pinewood security arrangements meant they had little to do. Kate left for the south of France for her Longines commercial. James said the main consideration was ensuring the Gaurige scenes, or carefully chosen snippets of those sequences, were inserted at just the right moments to reflect Asarov's inner feelings and ensure a perfect counterbalance to her developing relationship with Marx.

The conversation with James, Claire sitting with us in the editing suite, reminded me of the first time I'd read the script when I couldn't conceive how it could be made into a movie.

It is highly unusual, as Claire explained to me, for a director to edit their own films. She cited some examples of cinematic geniuses (the Coen brothers and Antonioni among them) who, either because of their obsessiveness or lack of faith that anyone else could fully realize their vision, insisted on full involvement at every stage of production. In fact, as I found out, James had been quietly editing during the entirety of the production, slowly bringing the project together as he worked. He had lived and breathed every part of *The Secret Writer* almost from the first day of filming. Rather than starting from scratch, he was in fact putting the finishing touches to the first full draft cut.

So, with four screens in front of him, James worked tirelessly and single-mindedly to pull the threads together. For example, as Viktoria takes her first tentative steps on her arduous journey from St Petersburg to London, James inserted just a moment, the tiniest fraction, of the Gaurige family celebration. It was a signal that the novel Viktoria was yet to write had already started to be conceived. Claire suggested one of Daniel's Gypsy characters be revealed as a foretelling of her meeting with Marx, but James disagreed. In his view, it was too early to show too much.

"After all," he explained, "Viktoria has not yet met him and I need to ensure it's layered in the right way. Alan took great pains to emphasize the importance of this. You see, Viktoria's novel is only starting to emerge and she hasn't yet had the opportunity to imagine her new acquaintances as the Gaurige family members—she hasn't yet met them! But hang on...you've reminded me of something absolutely crucial. Now that the audience has its first inkling of the great novel to come, although they'll have no idea what's going to hit them, we must be careful as we reveal the Gypsies. As Viktoria's experience and artistic frustration grows, she uses them as devices for her creative ideas—but we must synchronize it all perfectly."

The discussion raised further questions for me. Was there, in fact, something physical between Marx and Asarov, even though nothing had been explicitly revealed in the movie? Was there a relationship between Asarov and Engels that her sexual awakening was now pointing to? What about Engels and Jenny?

There was a knock at the door of the editing suite. Daniel Day Lewis entered and said he'd missed us all terribly.

"Nick, can I borrow you?"

Daniel took me on a surprisingly long walk from the editing suite through outdoor sets (one of which was for a Sir Kenneth Branagh movie about the building of Hadrian's Wall) to what looked like a long line of miniature airplane hangers. He took a key from his pocket and inserted it into a padlock that might have been better suited to a Charles Dickens novel. Noting my surprise at the ancient block of iron, Daniel explained it was one of many his father had collected over the years.

He pulled the door up to reveal something quite incredible. It was a ship, or sailing boat, the likes of which I'd never seen before. It was the boat Daniel would sail across the Atlantic Ocean, but was surprisingly small for a journey over such a long and treacherous stretch of water. It was only some five meters long. It had been fashioned from long, single pieces of timber that had been artfully curved so as to make a narrow bow, complete with a wooden Griffin looking out to the sea before it. All the way along the timber hull, Daniel had carved religious and heraldic symbols. In silent awe at the work, I ran my hand along them. Some were reminiscent of the Gypsy markings Daniel had fashioned for his caravan.

"I know what you must be thinking," he laughed. "I have to confess I took a little poetic license. Although the boat is based on medieval paintings, drawings, and plans I sourced from the Museum of Ireland, I couldn't help incorporating a few Gypsy influences here and there. I found out during my research the Romani had a strong impact on Irish culture and religion, stretching all the way back to the twelfth century."

Daniel asked me to walk around the boat, where I saw that the carvings had been mirrored on the starboard side. He urged me to move a little closer to the stern. In beautiful, gothic lettering, he'd carved the name of his masterpiece. The vessel had been named *The Secret Writer*.

I asked Daniel whether I could climb into the boat. He provided a small step ladder that he leaned against the hull. I moved to the center and put my hand against the mast. He'd carved a series of exquisite ornamental flowers and leaves along its entire length. I asked him what type of flowers they were and whether they were native to Ireland. I'd seen nothing like them before. Daniel asked me to look more closely and see if I could guess for myself. On closer inspection, I understood the miracle of Daniel's work. The mast carvings were not flowers at all, but rather an endless series of the letters S and W, decorated with flourishes and serifs.

"Daniel, I never would have realized! *The Secret Writer*, it's amazing!"

"Well," he replied, "it's my little trick and it can be our secret. It was just a bit of fun. I do hope you like it."

"I have to confess," Daniel mused as he abruptly changed the subject, "while I don't agree with all of James' ideas about film making, he has done an excellent job. And your acting, Nick...your acting is quite peculiar. I've thought about your performances many times. It's like you are always in character, but a character you can recalibrate for any situation. Take your Engels. When I see you, talk to you, and enjoy your company, and then compare you, now, to the Engels I worked with and have seen on screen, I can find no discernible difference. However, it is the strangest thing because your Engels is perfection—a perfect foil for Marx and exactly the type of intermediary required. I'm not sure how you achieved it. Your everyday life and your acting are a perfect match for each other. I thought I could teach you something about acting, but I find I have in fact learned much more from you than anyone I've worked with."

Needless to say I was humbled by Daniel's kind words, while not quite understanding what he was talking about.

Although I knew the answer to the question, I asked him whether he was serious about taking the boat from England across the Atlantic. It was inconceivable one man could safely manage such a journey.

"I'm sorry," Daniel said, as if waking from a dream, "did you say from England to America? No, I don't believe that's possible. And anyway the English, or Britons, never had the wit or skill for adventure. It's not their history I'm remaking! No, I will start the voyage from Ireland, as my forebears did centuries ago, from Dingle in fact. However, I will be at a distinct disadvantage compared to those intrepid sailors of the middle ages. I will be traveling alone which will make things a bit trickier! Having said that, I have constructed *The Secret Writer* at such a scale it will be easier to manage."

I cautioned Daniel against such an arduous journey. I couldn't believe he would put so much at risk. He put his hand on my shoulder to reassure me. Daniel was incredulous at my attitude.

"Nick, life is nothing if not about risk and adventure. You're one to talk! You threw caution to the wind when, surely, the idea of acting in a major motion picture must have seemed preposterous. You'd never acted before, but you instantly mastered your craft. You met and fell in love with Tilda Swinton. Nick, you risked everything and emerged victorious! It's the most inconceivable story, and one that almost rivals that of a young Russian who stakes everything on traveling to a foreign country to work for a Prussian philosopher! Yes, my friend, it's risky, but I've mitigated that risk by being prepared. I have built a solid boat that will not roll in even the most terrible conditions. I have designed a counterweight that is not unlike that used on Australia II when it won the America's Cup. So you see I am not throwing caution to the wind at all."

I was reminded of the risk mitigation strategies in the

change management plan the Executive Director had sent me. Each risk was labelled high, medium, or low and there was a description of how each would be addressed. I begged Daniel to install radio communications equipment. He laughed at my idea and asked where would the fun be if, at the slightest hint of danger, he could ask someone to rescue him.

"No, Nick, this will all rest on me."

After a second's pause, Daniel asked me a curious question.

"Nick, are you always acting?"

As I left his workshop, without answering a question that made me look inside myself and caused me to feel rather uncomfortable, Daniel asked whether I would care to have dinner with him. He wanted to eat again at the Viennese restaurant he, Tilda, and I had enjoyed so much. I said I'd meet him outside his workshop at six o'clock.

Some hours later, when I returned to the editing suite, James was still working the four screens. He was using a digital drag and drop editing program to splice different scenes together. It was interesting to watch him in action. He was identifying the right moment or sequence to pull into the master version on the screen to his furthest left. Claire was pointing and asking questions, suggesting an idea that would be dismissed with a wave of the hand or enthusiastically agreed to. It reminded me of the way Asarov and Engels worked together. James asked what it was Daniel had shown me. I told them about the sailing boat. James and Claire looked surprised when I told them the name of the vessel.

"I must say," Claire said, "that's quite a compliment to you, James."

"Yes, I suppose it is," he replied. "Nick, would you like to see the first part of the movie? It's rough, of course, but I think we are just about there."

James pressed a button that took the digital timer back to zero.

The screenplay was brought to life. The only visible parts of Asarov in that first scene were her hand and chest, the former desperately clutching at the latter as she died. A fountain pen drops to the floor, a candle is overturned, and we see thousands of pages of beautifully handwritten notes burning and turning into ashes. The scene, lasting five minutes and thirty-two seconds, ended with a close up of her fountain pen crackling in the fire before we are transported to St Petersburg where Viktoria is reading in the library.

It was another sixty-two minutes and nine seconds before Viktoria even arrived in London.

It was fascinating to finally see the realization of the film, or at least part of it. When reading the script, it seemed Viktoria's journey to London, as well as the scenes where the audience begins to understand this amazing young woman and her motivations, would be relatively brief. However, James had used this part of the story to carefully and gradually reveal Viktoria's character. Throughout the rail, coach, and boat journeys, we get a glimpse of her world, little by little, by way of a Gypsy dress, a violin, a kalinna detail on a caravan. He wove in moments of Viktoria writing with her fountain pen in her curious, gothic Cyrillic script.

I asked James whether it had always been the plan to render Viktoria in this way, or whether it had only occurred to him when he had sat down in the editing suite.

"Well," James said, "that's an interesting question. The layering was always the plan, as you noted the first time you spoke to me about the script, and I always knew we would have to do something to ensure the audience got to know that side of Viktoria. To be honest, the idea of revealing the Gypsy narrative in the earliest parts of the movie only occurred to me during the workshop with Alan. You remember, Nick, how we came to the idea you all play different Gaurige characters as a way of placing Marx, Engels, and Jenny firmly in Viktoria's imagination? Well it was a brilliant concept and gives the film, I think, a richness it wouldn't otherwise have. It was that very day I thought about exposing the Gypsy narrative much earlier so that both stories, set in different periods, one of which is 'real' and one of which is imaginary, unfold on top of each other, or side by side. By the way, why was Daniel so keen to show you his boat?"

I told them that Daniel was going to sail across the Atlantic for the Academy Awards.

I met Daniel outside his workshop. He'd attached a sail to the mast. It was dark green with a golden symbol in the center. Daniel said it was a triquestra, or Celtic Trinity knot.

"Anyway," he said as we sped to the restaurant, "I'm sorry for being a little short earlier. I'm hungry! By the way, the triquetra is an ancient Irish medieval Christian symbol. It seemed like a good choice given it was so commonly used on Irish ships. I commissioned it from a master sail maker in Plymouth and he's done a terrific job."

I agreed it was a beautiful design, and commented on the rich, emerald green.

"Yes, perhaps it was a little lazy of me to choose such an obviously Irish color but I couldn't resist!"

As we got out of the car outside the restaurant at its off-the-beaten-track location, I reminded Daniel how dangerous his ocean journey would be. I asked him to promise he would use navigational and GPS equipment, and maintain radio contact at all times. Daniel strongly resisted my advice.

"Nick, that would never do. If Irish sailors were able to make the journey many hundreds of years ago, and the Danes before that, then I'm sure I can manage it. The Atlantic can be unpredictable, but the boat is solid and will withstand just about anything. I appreciate your concerns but I need to be myself—there are so many times when I am not!"

As he laughed at his own joke, we walked up to the restaurant doors. However, although well-lit and apparently ready for service, it was closed. There was a note on the door. The owners had returned to Austria for family reasons.

As he peered into the empty dining room, Daniel said, disappointed, he'd very much been looking forward to a *jäger*. I was also hungry after a long day but the more pressing concern was how we would get back to our accommodation. I didn't know where Daniel was staying but I suspected he was sleeping in the workshop. His car had already driven away, but when I suggested he call his chauffeur, Daniel said we should walk. I protested it would take some hours to walk back along the remote country road. Daniel countered we would not take that route, but rather a shortcut through the woods. On the face of it, it was a sensible idea but even in the dark you could see the woods were thick with bracken and undergrowth. I was concerned we'd lose our way. Daniel laughed off any concerns I had. He had quite a deal of experience navigating by the stars.

"Remember what we were talking about earlier," he said. "Risk and reward! We will have our own little adventure."

Daniel asked whether I had seen *The Last of the Mohicans*. While I could only really remember the promotional poster,

I'm sure I had seen it on television at some stage. I knew the story and that Daniel had played the lead role of Nathaniel Poe. It had been included in the retrospective of Daniel's films that were part of the in-flight entertainment on our way to St Petersburg, but I hadn't had a chance to see it. Although unsure, I told Daniel I was familiar with the movie.

"Well then," he said, "you will remember it was largely shot outdoors, and often in rather difficult conditions. It took me many months to prepare my Nathaniel. I spent considerable time alone in wilderness areas of upstate New York so I could understand what it was like to travel long distances at night using only celestial navigation. Actually, although it's not often used these days, except by our Indigenous communities, it's easy enough to find your way using the stars as, if you like, sign posts."

Although reticent because I wasn't dressed for an outdoor adventure, I trusted Daniel and followed him into the woods. He found a large branch with which he slashed a path through the undergrowth. Every few minutes, he stopped and gazed up through the trees, often making a change in direction based on his assessment of the position of the stars. Just when I thought we might be lost and in need of help, we emerged from a thicket onto a street I recognized as Tilda's. I knew from there we could walk back to Pinewood or to the pub where Tilda and I had shared our first date. I noticed the lights were on in Tilda's house even though she was supposed to be in Scotland.

Daniel warned me not to approach. He said we should get back and find something to eat.

I couldn't resist the temptation. I crept up to the living room window and looked inside. Tilda was sitting in an armchair, naked. Sandro Kopp was painting her portrait.

As I looked through the window, I'm not sure why, perhaps I stepped on a branch or something else disturbed them, both Sandro and Tilda turned and looked directly at me. Sandro was holding his paintbrush as a drop of pale orange paint fell to the floor. The duration of their direct engagement with me seemed like hours, as if we were frozen in a photograph, even one of Sandro's portraits, but it was surely only a few seconds before they went back to their roles as artist and subject. Sandro's attention returned to the canvas while Tilda tilted her head, incredibly slowly it seemed, to its original position, looking slightly away from the artist to an undefined point in the middle distance.

Daniel urged me away from the window, whispering no good would come of staying here all night. I knew I should take his advice. Instead of heading back to Pinewood where our options would be limited to the cafeteria, we walked to the ancient pub where Tilda and I had first met and talked. He bought two pints of Guinness and two double Jameson's. His generosity went further when he revealed a sensitivity to my situation that surprised me.

"This life of ours," he said, "can be an empty one. In life you need anchors to ensure you are grounded and have a firm base to work from. Family, work, home, and routine are the things that make life easier to navigate. They give us certainty in unpredictable or troubling times. You see, Nick, you need a secure place to go where there are people you can trust and who you can either talk to or say nothing at all. I know I talk about risk and adventure, and I pursue both relentlessly because I understand the importance of challenging oneself. But remember, I do this in the context of having a firm family base to work from, and to which I can always return. Perhaps I am not so adventurous after all! Nick, you have left routine behind for a life that can be without certainty, and where people and their loyalty can be unpredictable. And I am not saying Tilda has been disloyal to you. We saw nothing to suggest any physical interaction between Sandro and her. In the world of performance you will find people are much more likely to explore themselves, and others, in a far more flexible and open way than you are used to."

I was touched, but troubled, by Daniel's sensitivity. In many ways, the structure he described as necessary to support the human condition reminded me of the restructure plan and, half jokingly, I said as much. Daniel thumped his fists on the table, causing our drinks to spill over.

"Exactly! Where is that report up to because it's been ages since I've seen it?!"

While initially it seemed he was trying to steer the conversation away from Tilda, Sandro, and the entertainment industry, I realized I was wrong when he asked a number of searching questions. I had to explain how the recommendations had come a long way from when he'd first seen them. I told him about the new approach to office accommodation and employee engagement, and how the former was supposed to improve the latter. I asked Daniel whether he wanted to read it, and he responded enthusiastically. I opened the document on my phone and passed it across the table. I am not sure about this, and never asked him, but I think Daniel Day Lewis is a speed reader. After just five or so minutes of navigating some seventy pages of text, diagrams, and charts, he was finished.

"You are quite right," Daniel said. "The recommendations have come a long way. Sadly, however, in my view they have gone backwards. I'm no expert in business restructure and corporate culture, I admit that, but I have worked on projects of considerable size and scope and dipped my toe into production. The initial work you did with Claire was practical and logical. It set out a long term vision but with short term, sensible actions that could be easily implemented. It didn't suggest radical change, but rather a gradual progression based on outcomes and key learnings. To be honest, this work just goes too far. You will lose people, valuable people, who may prefer to keep working in ways that have been productive and rewarding for them. You can't just front up to people and say what they've been doing for years has been a waste of time!"

Daniel had also absorbed the details on the new accommodation arrangements.

"This activity-based working," he observed, "is nonsense. Well, perhaps not entirely without merit, but how can you apply the same working conditions and environment to staff that have entirely different responsibilities and working requirements? You will have sales people, consultants, legal and administrative employees all trying to work productively in conditions that are plainly not going to be suitable for all of them. The overall plan is, I'm afraid, radical—but it's radically terrible!"

I felt the similar sadness I'd experienced when talking to Tilda about the report in St Petersburg.

"Daniel, you are right. Tilda and I came to the same conclusions when we first read the updated report and recommendations, but it was just after we received the news about Alan and we weren't thinking properly."

Daniel downed his whiskey, then his Guinness, and said the report had all the depth of a fashion magazine.

★

Should I relay Daniel's views to the Executive Director? Should I even bother? I agreed with Daniel the report had moved so far to the right that my input, and that of Claire, was barely recognizable. If I were to return to the firm I didn't think I'd like the new approach. Claire and I had identified, as Daniel had pointed out, synergies across the company. We had recommended simple steps to get everyone moving in the same direction, but I feared much of our thinking would be undone by a far more aggressive approach. Anyway, by this time we were leaving the pub and Daniel's car magically appeared to pick us up. He was dropped off at Pinewood, either to sleep or more likely to work on his boat. He kindly asked his driver to take me to the Manor House.

James, Claire, and Kate were sitting on the lawn enjoying a night cap. They were talking about Kate's modeling assignment for *Longines*. She'd been flown to Rome after a change of mind by the advertising director who had wanted to take photographs of Kate wearing the watches in the amphitheatre environment of Ostia Antica. The idea was to have a new theme for the advertising strategy—*timeless*. Of course, we all found the conceit amusing and laughed at the amateurish irony of describing a timepiece in that way. Kate outlined how the previous campaign, about elegance and, strangely in her view, horses, had not cut through as expected.

"It's a fine balance," she said, "between making sure the brand remains relevant but not overtly appealing to the mass market. They call them aspirational brands where sales figures and margins rely, against all common sense, on most people not being able to afford them."

I found the conversation underwhelming after the engaging discussion with Daniel. I had a lot on my mind. Even though just a few days earlier I'd been looking forward to spending time away from Tilda because I doubted there was any future in our relationship, having seen her with Sandro had caused me considerable distress. Then, having listened to Daniel's views on the report, I started to think Claire and I had wasted our considerable efforts.

But it was Tilda Swinton who really occupied my thoughts—her translucent beauty and searing intelligence would be lost to me forever. I went upstairs to my bedroom and was shocked to find her asleep in my bed.

Her skin had a fluorescence I hadn't noticed before. She was like a beacon. My attention was then drawn to an unframed canvas leaning against the bedside table. Only the reverse side was visible. I turned it over, being careful not to make any noise. It was a stunning portrait of Tilda. It was surely the painting Kopp had completed that evening. If anyone else had painted a naked woman in such a way it may have been obscene, but Kopp gave her strength, dignity, and vulnerability. Something caught my eye in the top left hand side of the canvas.

In the half-light it was hard to make out exactly what it was and so, not wanting to wake Tilda, I took the painting to the other room so I could more closely examine it. To Tilda's right and just above her shoulder, Kopp had painted a line of three picture frames. Given the striking nature of the portrait you wouldn't necessarily notice them at first—Tilda's grey-green eyes had a magnetic quality that drew you into position and kept you there.

The first was a tiny picture of an English thatched cottage. The one closest to Tilda's shoulder was of the Eiffel Tower. The object in between the two miniatures was slightly smaller. It was a mirror. In the mirror was the face of man. Only with my eyes a few inches from the canvas could I see that Kopp had painted me into the scene, reflected in the tiny golden mirror. I was looking at Tilda. She wasn't looking at the outer world from her armchair after all. No, she was looking at me, standing in the invisible foreground.

I was startled by Sandro's depiction of me and had no idea how to interpret it. Perhaps he was saying I was lost to Tilda, caught in some kind of purgatory, cruelly reminding me Tilda belonged to him, loved him, and my presence in the mirror or, more precisely, the fact I was forced to look at Tilda through the eye of the painter, was an eternal reminder he had won.

But there was another, more sensible explanation. I had been pulled into a world I could never fully be a part of. I was stuck on the periphery of everything, participating but never joining in. Surely this is what Kopp was trying to express. I was startled when my flame-haired actress put her arms around me. She had woken and managed to navigate the darkness without making a sound.

"Nick, is it not a charming portrait? At first glance I seem to be the subject, but look where the viewer's eye is drawn. Sandro has made that tiny image above me so intriguing you instinctively get as close as possible so as to discover what it is. And, my dear Nick, it is you! Yes, you are on the edge, on the periphery of the work, but that is how you hold yourself in the world. You are looking in but never quite belonging. All of us—Daniel, Kate, you, me, poor Alan—we all have this transparent and temporary quality. We affix ourselves to real or imagined characters for short durations, before desperately trying to find another. Why do we do this, Nick? I honestly don't know but it is the second oldest profession in the world, and surely the second most miserable. I feel I am always between things and never able to hold on to anything. That is until now."

All the time she'd been speaking her body was pressed up against my back, but with this last comment she turned me around so she could look into my eyes. It was a little awkward because I was still holding the painting. I extracted myself from her embrace so I could lean Sandro's portrait against the wall.

"Tilda, I agree with you in one sense but disagree in another. I understand the idea of in-betweenness, of the temporary, but for me acting is a *momentary* sensation of complete disappearance. I forget I have any life other than the one I'm playing, but nevertheless am able to return to myself as I need to. And I disagree it is a miserable profession. I enjoy losing myself."

Tilda suggested I hadn't been in the job long enough to understand. She pulled me into the bedroom where her desperation and ferocity surprised me.

When I woke Tilda was gone. She left a short note to say she was going to London to make a promotional video for Doctors Without Borders. As I walked past my bedroom window I saw Eric and Anthony playing badminton on the lawn. They'd erected what looked like a professional quality net, even taking the trouble to mark out the court with white tape of some sort.

Eric was serving. He launched himself into the air to gain maximum power, smashing the shuttlecock across the net before it rapidly slowed in mid-air. From the back of the court on the other side Anthony was no less agile. He hit his backhand at such an awkward angle his back was almost turned to his opponent. However, the height of his return gave him just enough time to re-position himself for Eric's drop shot, which Anthony was forced to dive for at full stretch.

The shuttlecock landed on top of the net, not able to make up its mind which way it should fall. Finally, it dropped to force Eric to make a shot and, impossibly, half his body in Anthony's court, he returned it, producing such depth that Anthony had to sprint to the back of the court and repeat his backhand feat of a few seconds earlier. It was an impossibly good shot and this time it was Eric who had to race to the baseline (surely he'd been expecting a shallow return) after having hauled himself from the ground. It was hard to tell whether Anthony's effort would fall in or out but Eric wasn't taking any chances. Running the short distance to the baseline he hit a reverse overhead that almost didn't make it over the net but, by some miracle, reached Anthony's side of the court.

The rally then settled into a more routine affair, both players moving each other around. They looked like professionals as they flashed their racquets at the shuttlecock, while ensuring they were well balanced for the next opportunity. Out of nowhere, having drawn Anthony to the net with an outrageous drop shot, Eric was nonetheless fooled by his partner who returned it with considerable interest. Perhaps the shuttlecock was caught by the wind but it sailed high and behind Eric. All he could do was hurl himself gracefully through the air and at full stretch return the thing just over the net. Anthony then had the simple task of cushioning it over while Eric was lying on the ground, mostly over the baseline.

They laughed, met at the net, and shook hands. It had been the last point of the match. They turned and looked up to my bedroom window. Eric waved.

When I went downstairs to make my way to Pinewood, the two strongmen were waiting for me. I offered my congratulations to Anthony, and said it must have been a tough game based on the few minutes I saw.

"We are very well matched," Anthony said, "and always have been ever since Eric taught me how to play."

"Now," Eric responded, "unfortunately he's become a better player than his teacher. I should have been more careful in choosing my protégé!"

Anthony laughed off the compliment, saying the reason he won the final set was because of the favorable wind conditions.

"It's not easy to play outside," he said, "and even though the breeze was only slight, it had a significant impact on the carry of the shuttlecock. I was fortunate to be playing that last set with the wind behind me."

Eric mentioned Kopp's portrait. It was the most beautiful portrait of a couple in love he'd ever seen. I had no idea how he had come to see the painting. By the time I arrived at Pinewood, Eric and Anthony close behind, James, Claire, and Kate were already there, viewing what looked like a draft cut of *The Secret Writer*.

＊

It was crowded in the editing suite. Eric and Anthony, no doubt keen to see the film and their portrayals of Gypsy characters, couldn't fit in the small room. Sensibly, despite our collective sense of anticipation, James called a halt to proceedings. He threw his arms into the air in frustration. He hadn't slept in days and there was a look of madness in his eyes.

"This is no way to watch a film! And where is Tilda and Elliot? Daniel? We will not watch the director's cut without the key players! We need to hold a proper screening. Even if it's as rough as anything, I will arrange for it to be transferred to print so we can watch it at the Pinewood cinema tomorrow. Claire, would you mind making sure Elliot and Tilda can make it? And Daniel also? Get him away from that bloody boat for a few hours."

We all agreed it was a good idea. The film required a larger canvas. Now at a loose end, Claire suggested we go out to lunch. Everyone nodded their heads in enthusiastic agreement. She wanted to try the Austrian restaurant she'd heard about, but I told her it was closed. Eric, from outside the editing suite, said there must be some misunderstanding because he and Anthony had come to know the family that owned the restaurant and they'd heard nothing. In fact, Eric informed us, it was open last night.

Eric said he would call ahead because *Der Wiener* didn't

usually open for lunch. He got out his mobile phone and we heard him laughing and joking, in German, with whom I presumed was the proprietor of the restaurant. It turned out one of the proprietor's sons had misunderstood a phone call from his father the previous evening. The son had thought he'd heard his father say *my uncle is very sick and we must go to Vienna (mein Onkel ist sehr krank und wir müssen nach Wien)*, when what he actually said was *it is getting dark and could you please go and buy some pears (es wird dunkel, und we brauchen mehr Birne)*. The boy had taken the initiative and affixed a sign to the door of the restaurant, thereby creating the misunderstanding that led to Daniel and me making our way home through the woods.

Claire must have got word to Daniel because he was already at the restaurant when we arrived. He had a giant beer stein in front of him. I couldn't contact Tilda. As soon as we were seated James tapped a fork against his wine glass. He wanted to say a few words.

I thought our director was about to make a long speech, but he spoke for only a few minutes. As he composed himself, looking like he needed a long rest and time away from the incessant pressure he had put himself under, I considered the impermanent nature of *The Secret Writer* project. The *writing* would go on forever but our closeness would dissipate as we moved on to other movies and relationships. I wasn't sure how much longer we'd be together. Surrounded by such talented people, my life seemed temporary, as Tilda had warned, stuck in a limbo of infinite sadness. However, I was quickly brought out of such thoughts by James' beautiful words.

"I feel so fortunate," he said, "because I have met each of you, and worked with you, to produce what I hope will be something beautiful. The film is the almost inaudible music of writing as it makes its way through the world. Viktoria," James looked to Kate, "scratches at her vellum and sends out her invisible magic. It continues to float through and around her by way of her imagination and her dreams. It is the invisible and almost silent friction the world would die without. All of us, collectively, are a vehicle for her secret writing and the revelation of her story, her life, and her death. Finally, let's drink a toast to Alan Rickman, without whom much of this imaginary world would never have been realized."

The lunch was otherwise uneventful. Each of us ordered the overly-generous jäger schnitzel. The flavor and color of the mushrooms had merged with the sour cream base, which had been seasoned perfectly. The veal was tender and delicious, while the rösti were crisp and lightly dusted in salt and sage butter. We were all drinking Riesling. It was dry, crisp, and well balanced. After we'd finished our veal, Daniel, who may have been a little drunk and couldn't stop mentioning the quality of the wine every time he took a sip, told an amusing anecdote of his time as an apprentice cabinet maker.

"I was as nervous as anyone in a new job, but especially so given I was entering a workplace filled with experienced men twenty or thirty years my senior. The workshop foreman told me to sand a raw piece of timber so it could be cut and used for a dresser or a desk or something. The timber was still covered in a thick layer of bark. I was told to walk to the store to buy super-heavy sandpaper to clean up the timber, and on the way back pick up tea and sandwiches for the rest of the team. It was a nightmare holding all these cups of hot tea, and sandwiches and sandpaper in a shopping bag! I nearly dropped the tea about five times. On my return, after having handed out the food and drink, I set to work sanding the timber. Although it seemed to me, even at that young age, a silly way of approaching the task, I set about sanding back the bark. After half an hour of working hard and getting nowhere, splinters all through my fingers, the men starting laughing. It had of course been a joke at my expense because I was the new apprentice. It was my initiation! The bark could easily be stripped by peeling it back by hand!"

As the laughter died down, the restaurant door opened and Tilda walked in. She urged me to come with her. I quickly finished my meal, drank the rest of my wine, stood up, and left. She almost dragged me outside. If anyone around the table was at all surprised by the commotion they didn't show it. There was someone she wanted me to meet.

As we got out of the car at the Manor House, a man stood up from his pot of tea (he had been sitting on the lawn under an umbrella) and turned to face me. His stature, both physical and otherwise, was imposing. He rose slowly, as if he were not one of the most influential figures in the history of American film but rather something resembling an ancient and majestic redwood tree. As he turned, the wizened face of Clint Eastwood came into sharp focus. He looked elderly but alert and he and Tilda embraced like father and daughter. Eastwood joked how he hated coming to England but if there was a good reason, it couldn't get any better than Tilda.

"Mr Eastwood," she said respectfully, "this is Nick Clement, an emerging actor. He has just finished his first feature film and I would be most surprised if you don't find his performance intoxicating."

"Well," Eastwood said, in a pleasant drawl, "it's a pleasure to meet you, Nick. Tilda has talked a little of you, and I believe she's mentioned a film project I am working on."

He spoke methodically, as if every word had been carefully memorized before his arrival.

"You may recall, Nick Clement, a film by the name of *The Seven Samurai*. You may not know it was directed by Akira Kurosawa in 1954. The film tells the story of a group of noble Samurai warriors who protect a village from tyrants. You may also know *The Seven Samurai* was adapted in 1960 in the

United States as *The Magnificent Seven.* It was essentially the same story but set in the wild west of America. It's an ancient tale of good against evil. Nick, I am going to make another version of this classic story. I won't revisit yesteryear, but reinvent it in the present day, in suburban Detroit, where the gangs have taken control. They *are* the law! A few honest men and women, and you will be one of them, band together, and make a stand."

Tilda couldn't contain her excitement.

"You see, Nick, it won't be a western after all. It will be incredible!"

I was honored to meet Clint Eastwood. I'd always enjoyed his movies and was terrified by Dirty Harry as a child. There was another, *Play Misty for Me,* a thriller, which was equally disturbing. I had seen *The Magnificent Seven,* but hadn't known it was a remake of a Japanese film. I wasn't sure what to say but thanked Clint Eastwood for thinking of me. I'd assumed he would be staying for the afternoon, or perhaps overnight, but instead he said farewell as his limousine pulled up.

"I don't expect an answer from you right now, Nick Clement," he said. "If you said yes straight away I'm not sure I could trust you. I want total commitment but I can guarantee you immense job satisfaction if you jump on board the locomotive!"

He walked slowly to his car, which was absurdly long, and bent his tall frame into the back seat. His chauffeur, having closed the door behind Eastwood, walked to the driver's side, all the time looking around as if wary of an impending attack. He was wearing an earpiece with a cord that reached inside his jacket.

"It is a great story," I said to Tilda, "and there is something to be said for watching a movie where you know exactly what's going to happen within the first few minutes. It's a comforting feeling. The project sounds interesting, and I like the idea of going to America, but I'm not sure it's the sort of thing I want to be involved in."

Tilda was horrified and couldn't believe an actor would pass on such an opportunity. She was furious and before she left asked *who do you think you are, Nick?*

I wasn't entirely sure.

Upon entering my bedroom I saw three paintings by Sandro Kopp had been hung side by side on the wall above my bed. On the left was his earlier portrait of me, the one he had sent to the Sachsenwald. The painting to the right was the Swinton that Kopp had completed a few days earlier. Between the two was a self-portrait. Most of the canvas was bare, with only a third of Kopp's face visible. Even that part of him appeared to be moving out of the frame, as if on his way somewhere. Kopp had artfully painted movement into the scene.

I didn't know who had hung the paintings but assumed

it was Tilda. I couldn't remember bringing my portrait back from Germany. The paintings were a triptych narrative of our time together. I realized the portrait of Tilda (with me in the tiny golden frame behind her) was reminding me I would only ever be looking in from the outside. The middle painting told me Sandro, too, would be ever-present but forever disappearing from view. Our relationship was fleeting and impermanent. I would never catch him. The portrait of me had, I saw now, rendered me somewhat transparent. While the paintings were engaging, I found the attempt to turn our relationships into a figurative narrative self-indulgent.

I could hear Eric and Anthony, the two constants in my life, playing outside, but the sound of the shuttlecock being smashed by the two strongmen stopped suddenly. It was replaced by a fierce argument. I walked to the window to see them standing over the same side of the court, pointing at the shuttlecock which had apparently landed squarely on the white tape. From the way he gesticulated and pointed, I could see Eric was convinced the thing had landed out but bounced back onto the line. I didn't know whether it was a crucial point in the match. They eventually played a let and got on with the game. I lay down and fell asleep. I dreamt of me, Daniel Day Lewis, and his boat.

We were in the middle of the ocean aboard *The Secret*

*Writer*, on our way to America for the Academy Awards. Although the weather was terrible with an endless series of rolling waves crashing on top of us, Daniel had the vessel under control. His long hair was tied in a ponytail and he stood upright, side-on, with both hands on the tiller. While navigating the stormy seas he issued instructions to tighten or loosen a rope, or move from port to starboard to improve our balance. The howling wind and crashing seas made it hard to hear. At one point he urgently told me to bring down the mainsail because it was about to get ripped apart. I was terrified I would be tossed overboard and lost forever, but somehow knew I would survive as long as Daniel was at the helm.

After a series of near catastrophes, the sea became calm. Night turned to day and the sun was beaming down. Daniel and I held each other in relief at our good fortune. We were approaching Cold Spring Harbor. On the shore, but a considerable distance away, was a young boy. Daniel kept his eyes on the point at which he wanted to bring the boat to ground and, while continuing to direct me to rearrange the configuration of the sails, navigated his way through shallow waters where treacherous rocks were visible below the surface.

He eased the boat onto the beach, jumped into the water, and waded through the shallows to pull The Secret Writer onto the sand. The boy had retreated. Daniel and I walked through the forest that bordered the beach, trying to keep up with this young fellow who flew across the ground with great agility. On several occasions we were so close we could almost touch him. The forest disappeared and we were at the start of a meadow that extended all the way to the horizon.

The boy appeared. He stopped and sat down under a tree. It was Luis Aragonés, the same boy we'd found many years in the future.

I must have slept for some sixteen hours, because I woke to Anthony calling through my bedroom door that it was nearly ten o'clock and we had to leave for the screening. Eric and Anthony drove me to the studio. It was the first time I'd seen Eric behind the wheel of a car. We were taken to a small theatre which looked like it had been built in the 1940s. The seats were covered in maroon velvet and there were matching curtains hanging from twenty foot ceilings. We were walking down the aisle when James called out. I hadn't noticed the rest of the group sitting in the back row—Tilda, Claire, Kate, Elliot, Daniel, and the director.

"We've been waiting," James called out, "please come and sit down!"

Eric, Anthony, and I turned around to join our colleagues, but because of the order in which we had entered the cinema, it was Anthony who slid in beside Tilda, Eric beside him, and me at the end in the aisle seat. Tilda reached over the two strongmen and touched me on the knee with the tip of her middle finger.

The lights went on and the curtains opened. There was a crude countdown from ten to one, and then some rudimentary credits that had clearly been added by the director himself. *Elliot Productions presents...a James McNeil film...Kate Winslet...Daniel Day Lewis...Tilda Swinton...Alan Rickman...and introducing...Nick Clemente.* The spelling error in my name could easily be corrected but I wondered whether it was intentional. The screen went black, then lit up with the words *The Secret Writer.* The font was a neat Garamond or Times New Roman.

We saw a hand, a fountain pen, a pile of vellum covered in handwritten notes. A crash, a broken glass, a candle falls over, the vellum catches fire, as do the curtains and, suddenly, the room is on fire. Then, a sweeping single aerial shot of St Petersburg taking us all the way into a dusty municipal library where Viktoria Asarov is reading, holding a clutch of literary pamphlets. We return to London and there I am, like a giant on the big screen, pretending to be Friedrich Engels.

*The Secret Writer* came and went in what seemed like minutes. We were reduced to silence. Elliot stood up and clapped his hands.

"This is the first and only time that I will sign off on a movie that lasts four and a half hours!"

It was hard to believe we'd been sitting there for half a day.

I can't explain why the film went by so quickly, except to say it was so engaging that time stood still. Interestingly, there was still no musical soundtrack, which I think made the experience all the more visceral. I remembered James saying musical accompaniment can remind the audience it's watching a movie and inhibit people from becoming totally absorbed in the narrative.

Apparently, it is very unusual for producers not to have a say over the final cut. They often have strong disagreements with the writers and directors, sometimes insisting on different endings, and cutting the film in length to make it more palatable to the general public. In the case of *The Secret Writer*, though, Elliot made it quite clear he didn't want to change a thing. Claire, being practical and pragmatic, suggested the film be screened to a test audience to gauge whether four and half hours might be too much. But Elliot leapt to the film's defence.

"No, no, no, no, no! It's a special case, a special cast, and an even more special story! I don't care what the audience thinks or even if no-one comes to see it. It is quite simply a masterpiece!"

There was a strange quiet amongst us, but looking back on everything I suppose it wasn't altogether an unusual reaction given the pressures and adventures we'd experienced. There was nothing more for us to do or create. Daniel was flicking through a National Geographic magazine. Tilda was looking at her mobile phone and Kate and James were holding hands.

I heard Kate ask him what they were going to do next. James said he'd written another screenplay he wanted her, and me, to read. It would be hard to follow *The Secret Writer*, but I knew there was only one person who could match it.

In the following weeks, having lost contact with him, I realized Daniel was somewhere in the middle of the Atlantic Ocean. All the time we were promoting *The Secret Writer*, I'd been worried. I imagined Daniel in heavy seas, managing the ropes and sails and looking to the stars for directions. I had seen first hand his ability to navigate in the darkness but in the middle of the ocean under grey skies, how could he possibly know where he was going? On more than one occasion I considered calling the navy, or the coast guard, but I knew Daniel would be furious. So, while navigating red carpet events, Daniel was always in the back of my mind. After a screening in Austin, Texas, I received a phone call. It was Daniel. His ship had broken up off the Island of Labrador. He'd managed to swim to shore but, having lost his wallet, needed me to buy him a plane ticket to New York.

I went to New York at the earliest opportunity. Daniel said the voyage had been fast and furious. Backed by a ferocious tail wind, the three-month journey had been achieved in a little over eight weeks. He was keen to hear from me, too, about reviews of the film and nominations. Daniel seemed unsurprised he'd been nominated for the best actor Oscar. He asked whether anyone else had been honored. I told him I was up for best supporting actor and Tilda likewise. Kate had been nominated for best actress and James for best director and original screenplay. *The Secret Writer* was also a candidate for best film. I didn't see Daniel again until the day of the Academy Awards.

The problem with being an actor is that disaster is always just around the corner. When you disappear into character you don't know what will be on the other side. That's what Tilda told me the last time we had any meaningful interaction. She was letting me go and it was understandable. We'd been thrown together and in the heat of the creative process we had perhaps let our guard down.

"You see," she explained, "you become the other. An *other* that is necessarily outside you but also *within* you. So, you could say you are either losing that self or, perhaps, you are tapping into an internal otherness. Either could be true," she explained, "but it's terrifying! Is there, for example, a part of me that is pure evil, without the faintest trace of humanity, who I can access when I need to? It gives me the greatest pleasure to reveal my evil self, if that is what's happening! Do I have such ill-feeling stored away inside me? Or, Nick, am I, are we, putting the self to the side, backstage as it were, and transitioning into a new self, if only a temporary one? It's a process—a virtual or real transition from one reality, the real, to another, where the latter, fictional reality must also *become* real for the transformation to be truly successful. But there are two sides to the metamorphosis. At the conclusion of the film, the play, the performance project, whatever it might be, you need to transition back to the other, parallel, *real* reality. Perhaps you could call it the personal or private realm. And what happens when you get back there? Well, Nick, it's an empty feeling. You have constructed another being, another character, something has been added to the world, but you are forced to leave that new personage behind. But stepping back to *yourself* in this way comes at a terrible cost. You *miss* those you have created. They become like a close friend you gradually lose touch with. It's like losing a family member who slowly recedes from memory so you miss them but can't remember what they look like. Nick, our lives are a slow disintegration and acting makes our understanding of that all the more acute."

I must confess, at the conclusion of *The Secret Writer,* while continuing to revisit the project at events and awards nights I, like Tilda, felt a great emptiness. I didn't know whether it was because of me, Friedrich Engels, or the Gypsy characters I'd played. I think it concerned the world I found myself in and the endless congratulations. James' work and vision was the real achievement. The rest of us were merely vehicles for his genius.

Adding to my feeling of aimlessness and loss was the fact that my relationship with Tilda had been, like our characterizations, falling apart. She was friendly but distant. She'd returned the Claddagh, placing it in the palm of my hand in a silent gesture of farewell. In the same way as Tilda had explained the acting process to me, I felt I was in the body of someone else. I felt smaller. After the initial thrill of building a character and seeing it come to life, I progressively felt diminished.

As the actors had suggested, this feeling of dissolution, of being between worlds, may have been because the project was over and I was experiencing the ultimate denouement. I knew if I continued to live in this environment I would slowly disappear until there was nothing left. Because I felt so unanchored I was determined to return to Australia as soon as I could. However, I decided to see the experience through to the Academy Awards presentation. I wanted to witness James' success. I also needed to see Daniel, who I knew would soon disappear from my life.

Daniel won an unprecedented fifth Academy Award. Kate won best actress. Tilda and I were unsuccessful, but James won the awards for best original screenplay and best director.

The party at Elliot's Los Angeles mansion went through the night. I talked to many people, but only for a few seconds before they moved on. Sadly, I spoke to Daniel only briefly. He had changed from the tuxedo into jeans and his maroon caterpillar boots. Tilda was singing Jay Z and Alicia Keys' *Empire State of Mind* with Ellen Degeneres. Eric and Anthony were tending the barbeque.

I was leaving long before the party would finish. Everything was in full swing as I walked out the front door, past the security guards, and down the long driveway into the street. I felt like walking. It took me nearly three hours to reach the hotel. I retrieved my passport and belongings, including the books given to me by Daniel. It was six in the morning when I arrived at Los Angeles international terminal.

On my way to the executive board room where Claire and I had presented in another lifetime, I noticed significant alterations to the working environment. Workstations had been replaced with open areas. There were breakout rooms for quiet work and team collaboration spaces. The printing room had disappeared. There was no need for any *RMFD780s* now the company had gone fully digital.

My meeting with the Executive Director and Chief Operating Officer lasted twenty minutes. Despite my protestations, they would continue to press ahead with the more radical changes. They again offered me a role in the new organization. I declined. They asked me about acting but I knew I wouldn't be seeking further work in that industry. I left the building, nodding to the few people I recognized, but I could tell they saw me differently now. There were plenty of new faces, many people having left the company, presumably because they'd lost their positions or decided the new way of working wasn't to their liking. As I walked through the automatic sliding doors, I received a text message from Tilda Swinton. I thought I'd never hear from her again.

Nick, she wrote, read this article.

I clicked on the link to the New York Times site. Daniel Day Lewis had retired from acting to become a cobbler in Turin.

# ACKNOWLEDGMENTS

---

I would like to thank Kate Kidman, Nick Whittock, John Hand, Melody Paloma, and Duncan Hose for reading (or being read) early drafts of Cinema. Lucy Moloney provided invaluable and expert editorial advice. I am most grateful for the faith and enthusiasm of Miette Gillette and WT, without whom this treatise on performance and being in the world would likely have found no other home.

# ABOUT THE AUTHOR

---

Samuel Kaye was born in Adelaide and grew up in Melbourne, London and Sydney. He now lives in Newtown, an inner western suburb of Australia's largest city. Kaye's first novella, The Circus, was published in 2014 by Inken Publisch. His short stories Jindabyne Holiday and The Turkish-German Girl have appeared in Sneaky Magazine. He has an Arts degree in English literature and languages from the University of Sydney, and a Communications degree in creative writing and philosophy from the University of Technology.

# ABOUT THE PUBLISHER

---

Whisk(e)y Tit is committed to restoring degradation and degeneracy to the literary arts. We work with authors who are unwilling to sacrifice intellectual rigor, unrelenting playfulness, and visual beauty in our literary pursuits, often leading to texts that would otherwise be abandoned in today's largely homogenized literary landscape. In a world governed by idiocy, our commitment to these principles is an act of civil service and civil disobedience alike.